"This one gets ten stars. It's the first book I've read by the Grey's, but I am now a fan. Their style is straightforward, with a good balance of romance, drama and suspense. I was so wrapped up in the characters and their story at the end that I was grinning and crying happy tears. I read a lot, and that is rare."
– *The Naughty List Reviewer*

"Wow, this story is a emotional roller coaster ride! It's a story of two souls who have lost their will to live and their encounter that gives them hope. This story is a real page turner, it's heartbreaking, soul mending and steamy."
– *Reading Keeps Me Sane Book Blog*

"Both characters are struggling with their own form of PTSD and I loved that the authors were sensitive to that. They introduced various mediums of assistance, therapy, pets, etc and I like that they are using reading as a way to break down some of those taboos. I loved this book. Its redemptive nature of the story and the power to be reborn after tragedy captured me. It was my first time to read the Grey's but I doubt it'll be my last. Bravo!"
– *Alphas Do It Better Book Blog*

"Will grab at your heartstrings the moment you open the book. A brilliant story about healing and acceptance that flows so smoothly that it hard to believe that there is two authors writing it. The chemistry is sizzling hot and the sex scenes should be read in private. I highly recommend you read this story, because you won't be disappointed."
– *Bella's Blog*

"This story just grabbed my heart and wouldn't let go… I had to grab the tissues early on so I knew this was going to be something unusual. I usually don't gravitate to 'make me cry' romance but this one snuck in under my radar and I'm so glad it did! I laughed, I cried and I got angry. This story hit all the right notes!"
– *Nerdy, Dirty & Flirty*

"Any book that can bring out my emotions this intensely will always get 5 Stars from me. This story ripped my heart out, and stomped it to little pieces. An emotionally charged, original, and well written story line flows effortlessly. The writing is so smooth that I always forget that there are two authors writing together. The off the charts chemistry, and SIZZLING sexy scene goodness should never be read in public. I'm quickly learning that Ozlo and Priya Grey can write anything brilliantly, with tons of emotion that brings tears to my eyes."
– *The Power Of Three Readers*

"A story about healing and acceptance. What started out as a stark, dark story eventually grew to one about healing and finding happiness again. I really loved this book."
– *A Wanton Book Lover Blog*

"OMG best book I've read all year. I laughed, cried like hard and felt hot and bothered. This is not only just another romance book this book is a book to show you s*** happens but let the people who love you to be your strength until you can see your worth of your life. IT'S A MUST READ."
– *Jassy Books*

"I really loved these two characters and their stories of emotional devastation. The emotion on the pages is almost too much to take in, but I promise you keep turning because it's worth it."
– *Ramblings From Beneath the Sheets*

HEALING MELODY

ALSO BY OZLO & PRIYA GREY

Awaken

Love's Composure

Love's Illusion

HEALING
Melody

By Ozlo and Priya Grey

Healing Melody by Ozlo & Priya Grey

Copyright © 2015 by Ozlo and Priya Grey. All Rights Reserved.

Print Edition: December 2016

Cover design by Ozlo Grey.

This book is a work of fiction. The names, characters, places, and incidents are products of the author's imagination and have been used fictitiously and are not to be construed as real. Any resemblance to persons, living or dead, actual events, locale, or organization is entirely coincidental.

The authors acknowledge the trademark status and trademark owners of various products referenced in this work of fiction, which have been used without permission. The publication and use of these trademarks is not authorized, associated with, or sponsored by the trademark owners.

All rights reserved. This book is published by BOA Press LLC. No part of this book may be used or reproduced in any manner whatsoever without the express permission of the authors or publisher. If you would like to do any of the above, please contact BOA Press LLC at boapress@gmail.com.

Printed by CreateSpace, An Amazon.com company

Published in the United States by BOA Press LLC.

ISBN: 978-1-940338-11-8

"In love there are two things—bodies and words."

- Joyce Carol Oates

1

KADE

I shouldn't be here – in an abandoned warehouse on the East Side of LA, fighting a dude ten years younger than me. I'm not ready for this fight. I didn't have enough time to train. The only reason I'm here – getting the shit kicked out of me – is because of my son.

Max is five years old.

I'm fighting to save his life.

Damn it! This sly motherfucker just hit me with an elbow strike. My right eye is swelling shut. Now, I only have one good eye to keep track of him. It won't be easy because this dude moves fast.

Figures, he's Brazilian.

Shit! He just hit me with another leg kick. My knee buckles. I struggle to stay on my feet.

Sensing an opportunity, the Brazilian storms forward and launches a spinning back kick. Losing my balance, I crash to the floor.

The crowd outside the cage roars with approval. They've come for a real fight. They want to see blood. Well, it looks like they're going to get what they paid for.

Unfortunately, most of the blood being spilled is

mine.

The Brazilian, whose name is Jose Silva, jumps on top of me and pounds me with a hammer fist. I thrust my pelvis forward to get him off of me. Quickly, I roll to my side.

But like I said: This fucker's fast.

Before I know it, he's got his legs wrapped around my waist. His arms squeeze my neck in a chokehold. By applying pressure, he hopes to cut off the oxygen and blood flowing to my brain.

This Silva dude has been fighting regularly for the last two years. He's good, real good. He's an expert in Jiu Jitsu and Muay Thai. He actually trained at my gym once. I taught him a couple of moves. I freakin' taught him how to properly apply the chokehold he's using on me right now.

Fuck.

I feel my head getting lighter from the chokehold. I picture my son, Max, lying in his hospital bed. He may only be five years old, but he has the heart of a tiger. He's been stuck in the hospital for the last month fighting what doctors' call acute myeloid leukemia. All I know is that it's a rare form of cancer. The doctor's are trying their best. It's going to be a tough battle.

Max is a fighter, though. He won't give up.

Neither can his old man.

I slam my elbow – hard! – into Silva's side. His grip loosens. I slam my other elbow into his other side. With a loud grunt, I fling my head back, and head-butt the Brazilian. He falls backward, finally letting me loose. Swiftly, I whirl around and try to place him in a neck crank. But he predicts what's coming and rapidly rolls away.

We both struggle to our feet.

I try to catch my breath.

This is the longest five minutes of my life. I just need to get through this round and hopefully get my second wind.

Through my one good eye, I stare Silva down.

I can't believe it. He doesn't have a fucking scratch on him. In fact, he looks like he just stepped out of the shower and is ready to go out to the club.

My chances don't look good the longer this fight goes on. I just don't have the stamina. If I had more than two days to train, maybe it would be a different story. But I can't use that as an excuse. Max doesn't need excuses; he just needs the best medicine money can buy.

That's why I'm here: Money.

If I win this fight, the money I'll take home will help pay for some experimental drug treatment. The doctors believe it may be the only chance Max has at beating the cancer.

I can't let my son down.

I lurch forward. I throw a superman punch at Silva followed by a liver kick. But he surprises me; he wraps his arm around my extended leg. Suddenly, he squats and punches me with an uppercut – straight to my groin. FUCK!!!!

I should have seen that coming. This is an underground fight. Anything goes.

No Rules.

There's no time to recover from the scorching pain

shooting through my nuts. Silva still has his right arm wrapped around my leg. I look up and see the sinister look in his eyes.

He's going in for the kill.

"Desculpa, velho," he says with a grin. Which means "sorry, old man" in Portuguese.

He flips himself over, taking my leg – along with my entire body – with him.

My head slams down on the mat. Silva then pins me in a knee bar, twisting my leg. Excruciating pain bolts through my lower extremity. He keeps applying pressure. I should tap out – quit – but I can't.

Max is counting on me.

Silva keeps twisting my leg. I struggle to get free.

"Tap out, old man," Silva screams in English. "I don't want to break it."

"No," I shout.

I won't tap out.

I can't quit.

I try to punch him, but I just hit the mat.

I hear the crowd outside the cage roar once again.

Silva keeps applying pressure and my leg bends further. The pain is unbearable.

I pray for a last burst of energy, hoping that I can somehow get out of this position.

"Tap out," Silva screams again.

I shake my head. "No!"

The pain burns through me like a raging fire.

I won't tap out, ever.

Then I hear the tear.

My leg snaps.

The fight is over.
I've failed as a father.
I'm sorry, Max.

2

Melody

I've been sitting at my piano all day. All I have to show for it is some shitty verse and a forgettable chorus. This song blows. I can't save it. It's terrible – just like all the other songs I've tried composing this week.

I ruffle my long brown hair. Then drop my head onto the piano.

I'm creatively fucked.

The record label has been waiting months for my new songs. My last album, *A Different Melody,* spawned five number-one hits and launched a sold-out world tour. I've performed to adoring fans all over the world: London, Rio, Sydney, Tokyo…

I'm the hot, new music sensation. My label doesn't want too much time to pass before releasing my follow-up record.

"We have to strike while we're hot!" my agent Randy keeps saying.

She checks in daily to see how the songs are coming. She says if the next album is as successful as the last one, I'll be bigger than Taylor Swift and Beyoncé combined. I think she's exaggerating but maybe not by much.

No one, including me, saw this kind of success coming.

In little over five years, I've gone from an obscure YouTube singer/songwriter to one of the most popular entertainers in the industry. And the funny thing is, I don't even put on much of a show. I don't dance on stage with an entourage, wear crazy outfits or even twerk. It's just me – my voice and my music.

But fans can't seem to get enough of me.

And even though I'm not much of an actress, it turns out fans like to see me on the big screen too. I've acted in two movies that have done really well at the box office. So besides being a successful musician, I also have a nice little acting career on the side. I guess you can say I've won the lottery: I'm doing what I love and everybody seems to love me.

But there's a problem: Now, everyone has expectations. I'm feeling the pressure big time to deliver on my next album.

In their last issue, *Rolling Stone* called me 'the voice of a generation.' Well, if that's the case, my generation is fucked. Because right now, every song coming out of my mouth is total garbage.

With my cheek still pressed against the piano, I dance my fingers over the keys. I'm trying to find some inspiration, but nothing's coming. I lean back on the piano bench and shout, "Fuck!!!"

My voice echoes off the walls of my living room.

Randy says if I'm having a tough time, she can call in some collaborators… aka ghostwriters. But that goes against everything I believe in. I write and perform my own music. If I sang someone else's words and tried to pass them off as my own, I couldn't respect myself. I'd be a fraud.

I look at my phone. It's almost midnight. I can't let another night pass without a decent song. I'm Melody Swanson for crying out loud. According to that same *Rolling Stone* article, 'I'm the next Lauryn Hill, the next Jodi Mitchell.' The way the article describes me, it's like I'm not even human: "Melody Swanson has the face of an angel and the voice to match. As the whole world anxiously awaits her next album, we can only hope it's as relevant as *A Different Melody*. If Miss Swanson delivers, then her status as musical juggernaut is assured. She will be a torchlight for these bleak times."

See what I mean by pressure?

I'm screwed! Every time I try to write a new song, I can't stand what I come up with. I just can't seem to get into a groove.

I can't be dried up already, can I? I'm only twenty-four.

Questions race through my mind.

Was my last album all I had in me? Was that all I had to say?

It can't be.

I need some inspiration, fuckin' pronto.

Should I meditate?

I tried that. It didn't work.

Should I roll another joint?

What's the point, the last one didn't help.

Should I get laid?

Now, that's something I haven't done in quite a while… but not by choice. My therapist strongly believes

I should abstain from sex for at least a month. She's worried I might become a sex addict on account of my escapades during my last tour.

You see, some people like to do a shot of whiskey before they go on stage, others, a line of coke.

Me: I like to fuck.

Sex unleashes something magical inside of me. It inspires me. And after a good round of fucking, I always feel extraordinary and want to take on the world like some sort of super hero.

And usually, after having sex, is when I write my best songs.

But my therapist, Jeanie, is really worried I'm developing a sex dependency problem. I told her she was full of it. So, she challenged me to prove her wrong.

"Go without sex for a whole month," she said during my most recent therapy session. "If you can do it without any trouble, then you don't have a problem."

She had me cornered, so I agreed.

I'm nine days into my abstinence. And it's a living hell.

Maybe if I just play with myself, I'll get inspired and write something good. But I just know there's something about a nice hard cock that always does the trick for me.

I drum my fingers on the piano.

Damn it! Now I can't stop thinking about cock. I really want a nice hard one buried inside me. I want to feel it driving in and out of my wet pussy. I picture myself wrapping my legs around the waist of a strong, muscled stud. I squeeze his firm butt as he plows me toward bliss. I'm getting so freakin' hot just imagining it.

This desire to get fucked is overwhelming.

Shit, maybe I do suffer from sex addiction.

But then I realize I'm dealing with extenuating circumstances here. I'm on a deadline. I have an album to compose and a career to sustain. The whole world is counting on me... or at least *Rolling Stone* is.

That settles it: Fuck abstinence.

It's time for a booty call.

I pick up my phone and quickly scroll through my contacts. My fingers stop instantly when Antonio Moreno's name hits the screen. I have a flashback to the hot sex we had after the Grammys. I remember running my hands over his flawless brown skin, over each clearly defined muscle. I lick my lips as I remember his cock. Damn, that drop-dead-sexy Dominican sure knew how to use it.

Antonio is one of the hottest Latin singers in the business, and also a very bankable Hollywood actor. He's not only good looking, but since he knows a thing or two about rhythm, he's also spectacular in bed.

Antonio is exactly what I need! As I dial his cellphone number, I hope he's in LA and not in Miami, his home base.

"Well, hello gorgeous."

My pussy tingles at the sound of his smooth and sexy Latin voice.

"Please, tell me you're in LA?" I breathe into the phone.

"That depends. What do you need?" he says calmly.

"You."

He laughs. "Melody, if you didn't have such an amazing ass and great pair of tits, I'd think you were a guy."

"Why?"

"Because all you want is sex and get straight to the point."

"It's the twenty-first century, Antonio. Women own their sexuality. Didn't you get the memo?"

"I guess I'm old fashioned," he responds. "I like leading the slow dance before I fuck."

"So, does that mean you're not interested?"

"Now, I didn't say that. Did I?"

"Great, come over," I reply with a wide smile.

"Now?"

"Yes, Antonio. Now. This is a booty call. That's how it works."

"But I'm already in bed."

I check the time on my phone. I'm surprised he's in bed this early. Antonio is usually a late night party animal.

"That's unlike you," I say. "It's only ten past midnight."

"I know," he complains. "I'm doing a guest appearance on *Criminal Element* tomorrow. My call time is 5 A.M… so," he says with a playful tone, "if you want what I can give you, you're going to have to come over to my place. But make it fast; I want to make sure I get my beauty sleep."

I hesitate. Antonio's been renting a beach house in Malibu, on the coast. I'm in the Hollywood Hills. Do I really want to drive all the way there just for a quickie?

"The clock is ticking, Melody. If you want my cock, you better hurry."

"Fine," I blurt into the phone. "I'm leaving now."

Ten minutes later, I reverse my blue Maserati out of the garage and drive toward the gates at the end of my driveway.

As I pull into the street, I notice an old, red Volkswagen Beetle parked a few feet away. That car has been there all week. I drive off, and in my rearview mirror, I see the lights of the beetle flick on. The car starts following me. Just as I suspected: Paparazzi.

I make my way down Nightingale Drive, toward Sunset. That red Volkswagen bug follows close behind. I need to lose it before I hit the Pacific Coast Highway and make my way into Malibu. The last thing Antonio and I want is our names linked in the papers. Especially since he's going through a bitter divorce in Miami involving the custody of his two kids. That wouldn't be good for either one of our public images. *Rolling Stone* called me an angel, remember?

I'm forced to stop at a red light. That red Volkswagen pulls up alongside me. The driver's passenger-side window is rolled down. I glance over and see a camera lens pointed straight at me. Behind the lens, I see a familiar round-faced guy with an unruly beard.

Fuck, it's him. I think his name is Charlie. He's the *WORST* of these LA paparazzi scumbags. He doesn't believe in boundaries. And lately, he's made getting footage of me his number one priority.

"Smile, Melody," he shouts. "Everyone wants to see a smile on America's Sweetheart."

I want to give him the finger. But again, I have an image to protect. I shoot him a stupid smirk instead.

"Don't you get tired of following me around?"

"You?" he replies with a grin. "Never. Now, Melody, why don't you tell us where you're going this Saturday night?"

I don't respond. Like I'm going to tell him. I need to lose this fucker, Charlie, before I hit Malibu. I take another look at his car and an idea springs to mind. The minute the light turns green; I'll slam on the accelerator. My Maserati will blow the doors off his old Volkswagen bug. Then, I can easily lose him in traffic.

I tap my fingers against the steering wheel, waiting impatiently for the light to turn. The whole time Charlie floods me with questions.

"Are you going to go see your boyfriend for a midnight rendezvous? Or is it a girlfriend? Come on Melody, the people have a right to know."

"No, they don't," I mutter to myself.

The light turns green and I slam my foot on the accelerator. From the corner of my eye, I catch a fleeting glimpse of something big and white. That's the last thing I remember.

3

Melody

When I open my eyes, I see a blinding bright light. Then, I make out a man's face. I don't recognize him. Through my blurred vision I notice a nametag on his white lab coat. It takes me a moment to read the letters. Finally, I manage to string them together: Dr. Mercer.

I attempt to ask him where I am, but I can't speak. That's when I realize there's a tube down my throat. I glance around nervously as anxiety rips through my body. I try to raise my head, but I can't move a muscle. A faint beeping sound quickens its pace.

"Relax, Melody," he says in a soothing voice. "You've been through a lot."

Relax. Where the fuck am I? What has happened to me?

Doctor Mercer turns and looks at someone. I can't move my head to see.

Fuck, am I paralyzed? Is that why I can't move?

"Now that's she out of the coma," Dr. Mercer says softly. "Administer 10 mg every four hours to help with the pain."

"Yes, Doctor," I hear a woman respond.

Coma? Will someone tell me what the fuck has happened? I

want so badly to yell from the top of my lungs.

Doctor Mercer turns and looks at me again. He offers a heartfelt smile but I can tell everything he's about to say will be devastating.

"You had a terrible car accident, Melody. You've been in a coma for two weeks. You suffered 3rd degree burns on over fifty percent of your body, including your face."

He continues talking but I stop listening.

Coma. Car Crash.
Third Degree burns. Fifty Percent.
My Face!

Dr. Mercer finishes talking and gives me another warm smile.

"We're going to get you through this," he says reassuringly before stepping away. As he leaves, my eyes overflow with tears.

Once he's gone, a nurse appears in my vision. She concentrates on the IV pump next to my bed. As she adjusts a setting, it beeps. Then she glances down at me. I see the pity emanating from her eyes. With a soft, sad smile she takes a seat beside me. I see a needle in her hand. She pricks my skin with it. As she pulls back on the plunger, she says, "This will help with the pain, sweetie. I'll come back to check on you in a bit."

What pain? I can't feel a thing. I'm numb.

The nurse leaves the room. She draws all the energy out with her.

Chilling, scary thoughts ricochet through my mind. How did this happen to me? Why did it happen? Dread and shock sweep over me. I want to throw my hands up in the air, scream and cry all at once… but I can't move. I can't feel a single muscle in my body. The air around me recedes. I'm trapped. Trapped in a badly burned, damaged body. This can't be real? It's a nightmare. That's what it is, a nightmare. I just have to wake up.

But then I begin to feel the pain. This pain is real. It's not a dream. My body is suddenly wracked with it. Tears of agony fill my eyes. Then, thankfully, I feel an unfamiliar, warm sensation run through me. The pain subsides. It must be the drugs the nurse administered. Slowly, a soothing feeling washes over me. My eyes get heavy and I begin to fall asleep.

When I wake up, my nightmare continues. For the rest of the week, I'm in a drug-induced fog as Dr. Mercer and several nurses try to manage my pain. Slowly, I am able to piece together what happened the night of the crash. Images assemble themselves together like a jig saw puzzle, creating a devastating memory that loops in my mind over and over again. They hit me like flashes of lightening: my foot slams on the accelerator when the traffic light turns green, a white truck flies out of nowhere, the truck t-bones my Maserati, my car spins into oncoming traffic. The windshield shatters, the glass prickles my skin. I feel the weight of something hard, and cold as metal, press into my side and face. Everything around me fades to black. When I regain consciousness, a wave of heat engulfs me. Fire. The car is on fire.

I'M ON FIRE!

I recall trying to scream as the flames scorched my skin.

"Help Me! Help Me!" I tried to shout. But the words just wouldn't come out.

I swear I have a blurred vision of him: Charlie – that fuckin' paparazzi guy with the beard. He stood a few feet from my car... taking pictures. He photographed me while I was helpless and burning to death.

As the red-hot flames licked my skin, the pain became unbearable. I blacked out again.

Now, here I am. Four weeks later, shackled to a hospital bed, supposedly lucky to be alive. My jaw, nose, and cheekbones were damaged in the crash; in addition to my face and body being badly burned. Because of all the injuries I sustained, doctors had to repair my jaw and reconstruct part of my face. Now, I'm wrapped in bandages like a mummy. Doctor Mercer says it's going to take several reconstructive burn surgeries to get my face and disfigured skin back to some semblance of normalcy. And in all likelihood, I won't look like I did before the accident.

So much for having the face of an angel? It sounds like I'll be the newest attraction at the circus freak show.

Dr. Mercer also says I should expect at least a year of physical therapy to get back to my normal movement and body function. Apparently, I should be grateful I'm not paralyzed.

Why does everyone feel the need to tell me how I should feel?

How did this happen to me? I guess that's a stupid

question. It happened because I was trying to lose that paparazzi asshole and got t-boned by a truck running a red light.

I guess the real question is why?

Why did it happen?

Why did it happen to me?

I've always believed in God. But how do I wrap my head around this? Why would God hurt me? I'm Melody Swanson. I'm supposed to be the 'voice of a generation'. I'm supposed to have the face of an angel. Why would God punish me? Why would God take away my face and destroy my career? I thought I was doing something good with my life, giving people a gift through my music. Then why would God decide to take that all away?

Because of this accident, my career is over. I'll never be able to step on a stage again. I'm going to look like a mutant for the rest of my life. I thought I was put on this earth to entertain people; now they're going to cringe at the sight of me.

I know I'm not a saint; but there are a million assholes in the world. That paparazzi motherfucker, Charlie, is a perfect example. Why didn't this happen to him? Why didn't *his* car get smashed? Why am I the one who's stuck in the hospital? Why is it *my life* that is forever changed? Why is it *my career* that's been snatched away?

Why?! Why?! Why?!

Maybe God hates me… I wish I had died in that crash. I can't find any good reason to live like this.

One thing is for sure. My body may have survived, but my soul has passed away. My music is gone; its spirit has abandoned me. I can feel the empty void it left behind.

I'll never sing or perform again.

If that's my reality, what's the point of living?

If I could move my body, I'd destroy this hospital room in a rage. I'd smash everything in my sight. ARGH!!! I'm so fuckin' angry! So filled with venom! But all I can do is lay here, like a corpse.

I don't want to live anymore if it means living like this… permanently scarred, my musical spirit crushed.

When I get out of this hospital, I'm going to kill myself. There's no point in going on. I don't see a future for myself anymore.

The thoughts racing through my mind are halted when I hear, "I'm so sorry." Suzie takes my hand in hers. I see the tears in her eyes as she looks at me. "I can't imagine what you must be feeling right now."

If I could move my jaw freely, I'd tell her I'm angry, and depressed, and numb all at the same time. It doesn't make sense. None of this makes sense. But I can't talk; all I can do is look at her. Suzie is my personal assistant… and also my best friend.

Can Suzie see the fear in my eyes? I think she can.

She lowers her head and shakes it. "I don't know what to say, Melody. All I can tell you is that I'm here for you, okay?" She looks at me and smiles. It's a genuine, heartfelt smile. I'm grateful she's here.

I feel the tears stream from my eyes. I manage a slow nod.

Suzie then gently squeezes my hand. "Listen," she says. "I know you're not going to like this, but your parents are outside. They want to see you one more time."

I instantly roll my eyes. Suzie nods. "I know, but they insist. Randy is out there too, so is Nancy. I've held them off as long as I can but they want to see you now. Okay?"

Although I'm not in the mood for visitors, I realize I don't have a choice. I slowly nod my head.

Suzie gives my hand another squeeze and then stands up. She wipes her eyes and walks to the door. They all rush in: my parents; my agent, Randy; and my publicist, Nancy. They immediately surround my bed.

They make several comments that I can't reply to. All I can do is stare at them and nod here and there.

"You're lucky there was a patrol car in the vicinity," my Mom says. "Officer Mendocino arrived just in time to pull you out of the wreckage." She's a broken record. My mom has already mentioned this several times on prior visits but feels compelled to say it once again.

I wish my parents would just fly back to Cleveland and leave me alone. All they keep saying is how lucky I am to be alive. That's all anyone says. I wish everyone would just stop. I'm not lucky. I'm fucked. Now, please leave me alone.

"Baby, I know things look dark right now," says my father in a worried tone. "But you're going to pull through this. It's just going to take time and patience."

I want to laugh at what he just said, but can't.

You have no idea what I'm going through, I want to say. *And I'd rather be alone than look at the uncomfortable expression on your faces as you stare at me.*

"I'm going to come by tomorrow with your iPad, so you can watch some movies," Suzie says. I can tell she's fighting back tears as she stares at my bandaged face.

"The label says they'll cover all your medical bills, including plastic surgery," chimes in Randy, my agent.

"That's awfully nice of them," says my mom.

Again, I want to laugh. My last album was the reason the label hadn't filed for bankruptcy. Paying my medical bills is the least they can do.

"And I spoke to Jack, the president," continues Randy. "And he said anything you need, you just let him know."

A new body would be nice, I think to myself.

My publicist, Nancy, who is standing off in the corner, takes a few steps toward the bed. She looks at my parents. "I think when we're done here, one of you should talk to the media. Tell them about Melody's recovery."

"I'll do it," replies my mother with a serious nod.

"I'll be by your side," says my dad.

"Great," replies Nancy. "I'll write something up for you." Then, she glances down at me. "Melody, is there anything you would like the public to know?"

"She can't talk!" snaps Suzie. "Her jaw is wired shut, remember?"

"Right," says Nancy with a curt nod. "I'm sorry. My bad. I'll be back with a statement." She nods to my parents and walks out of the room.

Once she's gone, the rest of them just stand there, surrounding me, not knowing what to say.

"You're lucky to be alive," my mother mutters once again.

I'm not lucky.

4

KADE

The hospital lobby is swarming with reporters. Security is yelling at them to vacate the premises. As I ride the elevator to Max's floor, I overhear two nurses talking about some pop star that just got admitted. Car crash. One of the nurses asks the other if it would be inappropriate to ask for an autograph.

As I step out of the elevator, I use my crutches to make the long journey down the corridor to Max's room. I don't know how I'm going to face him, knowing I failed him. When I enter the room, I see my older sister, Layla, standing by his bed. She glances at the brace on my right leg and immediately knows I lost the fight. Her face darkens with sadness. I hobble over to the bed. With his eyes half closed, and his face pale white, Max looks at me and tries to smile.

"How's my little tiger?" I say, touching his cold hand.

"Did you beat him, Dad?" he softly asks, his voice as weak as a whisper.

I can't tell him the truth: That his father has let him down.

"You bet I did," I lie, forcing a smile.

Layla, who stayed with Max while I was at the fight, looks at me with caring eyes.

"He refused to go to sleep until you came back," she says. She then gently squeezes my shoulder.

"I knew you'd beat him," Max murmurs, struggling to keep his eyes open. "You're the toughest guy on the planet."

I have to use all my willpower to keep from crying right there in front of my boy. It requires more strength than the fight I was just in. I take a deep breath and nod.

"You know it, Tiger."

"Dad, when am I going to leave the hospital? I've been here forever."

"Soon," I reply. "We just need to make sure you get all better." I gently squeeze his small hand. He's so delicate. His arms, razor thin.

"Why's it taking so long?" he asks, looking up at me.

I'm at a loss for words. I look at Layla. I can tell she doesn't know what to say either. How do you explain to a five year old boy that he's sick and we're doing everything we can to make him feel better, but it might not be enough? I look into my son's weary, young eyes and sigh. "Max, you know how sometimes we go out for ice cream, and you like to try all the different flavors to see which one you like?"

Max nods.

"Well, that's what the doctors are doing with your medicine. They're trying to find a medicine that your body likes. It's just taking a little while, but we'll find it. I promise you."

I'm on the verge of tears, but I force myself to keep

them at bay. I smile at my boy as I gently run my hand over his head.

"I miss mom," Max utters softly.

Layla and I share a silent glance. I don't know what to say. The beeping sound from the monitor resting near Max's bed echoes throughout the room. Max hasn't seen his mother in over three years. She abandoned him. The pressure of being a single mom while I was away fighting in the Middle East was too much for her to bear. To cope, she began drinking and doing drugs. When I returned home from my last tour of duty, I saw the destructive state she was in. I told her she needed help, but she refused to seek treatment. Then one night, she disappeared. Max and I haven't seen her since.

"Honey, you just focus on getting better," says Layla. She caresses Max's thin arm. The illness has consumed his fragile body.

Since Max's mom left him, my sister Layla has stepped in to help me. "Now remember what you promised me," she reminds Max. "When your daddy came back, you promised you'd go to sleep. Time to rest those tired eyes, sweetie."

"Tigers need their rest, Son." I tell him that every night at bedtime.

"Okay," Max says quietly.

He offers me a soft smile and closes his eyes. Within seconds, he's fast asleep.

Layla looks at me and whispers, "Let's step outside."

I follow her into the hallway with my crutches.

"He's getting so thin," I mutter once we're outside the room.

My sister nods. We remain silent as people race back and forth down the corridor.

Then Layla finally speaks. "I think you should try and find Monique."

I look at her dumbfounded. "Are you kidding me?"

My sister shakes her head. "She has a right to know."

"No, she doesn't," I snap, loudly.

Layla sighs and looks around at some of the nurses and doctors in the hallway. I move in closer and remind her, "She deserted him."

"But she's his mother," responds Layla. "And you heard him. He wants to see her."

Now it's my turn to sigh. I know she's right. But the last thing I want to deal with is Monique. "I don't even know where she is," I gripe.

"But you know people who might," replies Layla.

"Maybe."

"Listen," she says, changing the topic. "Doctor Wang stopped by while you were gone. He said the last blood test showed his t-count is getting lower."

"Fuck," I reply, shaking my head.

Everything is going from bad to worse. My Max doesn't deserve any of this. Why couldn't I be the one struck with cancer? Why him? It's not fair!

Layla continues. "Doctor Wang asked if we discussed the experimental treatment he mentioned? He said we should make a decision soon. Max's body is deteriorating at a rapid pace."

I feel a strong knot of anger growing in my chest. I stare at my sister, frustrated. "I already made my decision, Layla. There's just one problem: How am I going to pay for it? This new treatment isn't covered by insurance. I'm maxed out on my credit cards. I've borrowed all the money I can against the gym."

That knot in my chest is now a massive lump in my throat as I realize I might not be able to pay for my son's treatment – a treatment that might save his life. How could I let him down like this? I glance at my broken leg, then at my crutches. I'm a fuckin' failure. I couldn't even win the fight for my son's life.

Layla places a hand on my shoulder. "I'll ask Marcus if we can borrow more money against the house –"

I shake my head, cutting her off. "No. You two have already helped out more than enough. You have your own family to look after."

"You and Max are part of my family," she replies. "I'll do anything for you two."

Her generosity makes me want to cry. Even if Layla and Marcus could get a second mortgage, it wouldn't be enough to cover all the medical expenses. I look down at the floor, defeated. I take a huge breath and try to shove the lump in my throat back down into the pit of my stomach. I remind myself I need to stay strong. But I'm barely keeping it together. "Thanks," is the only thing I manage to say.

I gather the courage to look my sister in the eyes again. Then, I describe to her exactly how bleak things appear.

"I was doing some research, Layla. Even if this treatment works on Max, it doesn't mean he's in the clear. There might be a lot more treatments involved." As I talk, the emotion I've been trying to suppress slowly bubbles to the surface again. I've been trying to hold myself together, but I feel like I'm about to break. "I want to do everything in my power to save him," I confess to her. "But I'm failing."

I smack one of my crutches against the wall. Then I glare at my sister, seething with self-loathing. "I wanted to win this fight so badly, Layla. But I couldn't even do that. Even though I was fighting for my boy's life, I could not win the fight." I try to calm down but I can't. Hot tears stream down my face. "I would have died in that ring," I cry, "if it meant Max could walk out of this fuckin' hospital, healthy."

I take a deep, long breath.

With a sigh, I add, "It all comes down to money, Layla. And I don't have it." I look at her and confess the sad truth. "Even if you and Marcus take out a second mortgage on your house, it won't be enough to keep Max alive."

I look back at the floor. I feel like I'm suffocating from the pressure coming at me in all directions.

"Hey," snaps Layla. She grabs my head with her hands and looks me squarely in the eyes. She speaks to me with a strength I wish I could manage at the moment. "You can't lose faith, Kade. You hear me? You never lose faith. So you lost this fight and got a busted leg. It doesn't mean it's over. We'll figure out a way to get Max what he needs. You hear me?"

I nod slowly.

"Yeah," I mutter, although I'm having a hard time keeping my faith right now.

Layla straightens herself. "Okay. Now stay strong." She

adds, "I'm going to the cafeteria to get a cup of coffee. You want one?"

I nod.

"I'll be right back."

I grab her arm before she has a chance to walk away. "Thanks," I tell her.

She looks at me with a sad smile. "For what? Being an older sister?"

I nod. "Yeah. I'm grateful I've got you by my side." I pull her into a bear hug.

"Don't mention it," she says with a tender look. I release her and she walks toward the elevators down the hall.

Once she's gone, I lean against the wall and close my eyes. I breathe deeply and slowly. I need to get myself together before entering the room again to see Max. I have to look strong when I'm in his presence. He can't see me in this emotional state. It would just fill him with worry, and that poor kid has enough to deal with. That being said, I still have to figure out how to pay for Max's treatment. Where the hell am I going to come up with that kind of money?

"Am I coming at a bad time?"

I open my eyes and see Shane standing in front of me. His two bodyguards, Vince and Leo, hover a few feet from us.

5

KADE

"I thought I'd come by and see how the little guy was doing," says Shane.

Shane and I are childhood friends. We grew up together in the ghetto of Westmont. We used to be thick as thieves – until Shane actually became a thief. He was always attracted to the quick buck; and by the age of sixteen, he was running his own gang, committing burglaries and dealing drugs. I didn't agree with his life choices, but I remained his friend.

I even took a bullet meant for him.

It happened when we were teenagers. We were hanging out on the front lawn of a house party. A rival gang must have been tipped off about our location. Out of nowhere, a car sped down the street. When I saw a gun pointing out the car window, I immediately ducked and took Shane to the ground with me. I got shot in the side. Luckily, the bullet didn't hit any organs. After a stint in the hospital, I was okay.

Shane couldn't believe I took a bullet meant for him. I couldn't either. On instinct, I just wanted to protect my friend. But that night, as I lay recovering in the hospital,

I realized I needed to get out of the ghetto. I wanted my life to have meaning. So, I enlisted in the army.

Going to war changed me.

When I came home – between tours – I slowly realized I wasn't right in the head. Everywhere I turned, I felt the possibility of danger. I couldn't be in crowded places, and driving my car on a busy street always put me on high alert. I was angry most of the time and would lose my temper in a second. I didn't realize it, but I was suffering from PTSD. Instead of getting help, I just went back to Iraq.

I felt more comfortable being in the Middle East than at home in LA.

That all changed when I came back from my last tour. I saw how badly Max's mom, Monique, was doing. Her drug addiction had escalated. I realized then, even though my regiment needed me in Iraq, my son needed me to stay home. So I stayed… to be the father I wished I had been all along. Max moved in with me and I turned to MMA fighting to help support us. And fortunately, with some of my winnings, I opened up my own gym – Kade's Cage.

Shane's life took a much different route. While I was off fighting in the desert, Shane hustled the jungle of LA. He was always a smart guy – maybe too smart for his own good – and worked the streets to his benefit. In little over three years, he became a major figure in the LA criminal world.

And today, he has his hands in all sorts of rackets – from drugs, to prostitution, to underground fighting. He's gone from being a ghetto kid, just like me, to a "businessman" who wears thousand dollar suits and expensive diamond stud earrings.

But when you're at the top of the food chain, a lot of people want to take you down. So, Shane has his bodyguards – Vince and Leo – with him at all times. They're big burly guys who might as well be cut out of stone. They show no emotion. They're as cold as ice.

When I came back to LA for good, I tried to leave the war behind me. Shane, on the other hand, has been fighting his own war since he entered 'the life' at the age of sixteen. His life is always at risk. But I think he likes it that way. It gives him a rush. Since I've been back, we're not as close as we used to be. Shane's been busy building his criminal empire. But that's not the only reason. The only thing Shane values these days is money. He has no room in his life for old childhood friends. That's why I'm surprised to see him here.

"He's sleeping," I tell him. "But you can come in and see him."

I turn and hobble into the room. Shane follows me. His bodyguards wait outside.

Shane can't hide his shock when he sees how sick Max looks. "Damn," he mutters.

"Yeah," I reply.

We stand in silence – both Shane and I – virile, strong men staring at the ravished, sickly body of my son.

"How's the leg?" Shane eventually asks.

I shrug. "Broken."

"I heard you didn't tap out?"

"I couldn't."

Shane stares at me for a moment. I can't tell what he's

thinking. He then sighs and walks out of the room. I follow him. When we step into the hallway, he reaches into his suit pocket. He takes out an envelope and hands it to me.

"Here's your take from the fight."

I take the envelope and open it: two thousand dollars. If I had won, the take would have been seven thousand dollars. Still not enough for my son's treatment. But it's a start.

Shane turns to Vince and Leo and tells them to give us some space. The two burly bodyguards nod. Shane then walks down the hall and motions me to follow. I sigh as I try to keep pace with him on my crutches.

"The lobby downstairs is crazy," he says.

"Yeah, I think there's somebody famous staying here."

"Melody Swanson," he replies.

I look at him and shrug. The name doesn't register with me.

"You know, the singer?"

I shake my head.

"Dude," he says. "Her songs are all over the radio. She was in that movie. That chick flick with that guy; I forget the name of it."

"I don't watch chick flicks," I say offhandedly.

"I don't fuckin' either," says Shane. "But the billboards for it were everywhere. I think her car exploded or something. I heard one of the reporters say she's fried chicken. Anyway, who gives a shit." Shane points at me and says, "You should have tapped out, Kade. Now, you're out of commission for at least five months."

"You're probably right," I agree, not really listening to

him.

My mind is elsewhere – on Max.

Shane stops and turns to me. He looks me up and down.

"Hey, I understand why you didn't," he says. "He's your son. I get it. " He continues walking, and I hobble along. "Either way," he says. "You made quite an impression. I think once you're all healed up, we can schedule you for another fight. Bigger take next time. How's that sound?"

"I'm not sure the result would be any different," I admit. "I need to spend more time training and with everything…you know, with Max…it's tough."

Shane looks at me and nods. "Yeah, I know. How you holding up?"

I stop and take a breath. I straighten up and look at him. "I'm holding."

We stare at each other for a moment. Shane's not a big talker and neither am I.

"Listen," he finally says, glancing down at the floor. "I've been doing some thinking about your situation." He sighs and shrugs. "I've never forgotten about that bullet you took for me when we were kids."

I nod.

He continues. "And I know you need a ton of money for your boy's treatment. I have an arrangement that could work for the both of us. If you're interested…"

I don't know what to say. The tension I've been carrying in my chest and stomach eases for the first time in weeks. I'm overcome by a foreign feeling, a jolt springing my body back to life: A sense of hope.

"What?" I ask, unable to control my smile.

Shane motions me to continue walking. I hobble along, but I'm excited now, energized. I might be able to save Max's life!

"Now, I've got to warn you," says Shane as we continue walking down the hall. "You might not like it at first."

"I'm listening," I say, unable to hide my enthusiasm.

"You know guys like you – vets? It turns out you're quite popular."

"That's news to me," I reply. "Nobody seems to want to hear about us when we get back home. We're just forgotten."

"I'm not talking about any of that," says Shane. He stops and looks at me. "It turns out there's a demand for guys with your background and with your looks." He moves in closer and lowers his tone. "I've started a side business that's making me a ton of money – a lot of demand and not enough supply. I'm thinking you can help me out in that department."

I'm not sure what he's talking about. But honestly, I don't care. I'll agree to anything if it means saving Max's life.

Shane leans back and looks me straight in the eye. "You agree to help me out," he says. "And I'll cover all of Max's medical expenses."

I don't know what to say. My prayers have been answered. Hallelujah!

When Layla steps out of the elevator with two cups of coffee, she's surprised to see Shane and his two bodyguards standing in the hallway.

Shane smirks as he admires my sister in a long, lustful gaze. "Hello, Layla. Looking as beautiful as ever."

"Thanks," replies Layla in a flat tone as she walks past them and toward me. She hands me my cup of coffee. She then turns and watches as Shane and his men step into the elevator and disappear.

"I've never liked him," she says. "What did he want anyway?"

I don't answer her. My mind is still spinning from my conversation with Shane. I take a sip from my coffee, trying to process it all. Shane might have been my best friend growing up, but I feel like I just made a deal with the devil.

"Kade, what did he want?" repeats Layla.

I finally snap out of it. "He offered to help with Max."

Layla looks surprised. "How?"

"He'll pay for all the treatments."

Layla's expression slowly changes to one of suspicion. "In exchange for what?"

6

Melody

One Year Later…

"I need you to increase my dosage."

"You're already taking a pretty high amount."

I eye my therapist coldly through my mask. "It's not enough," I say. "I still can't get any sleep."

"Nightmares?" she asks, staring at me through her glasses, her notepad flipped open on her lap.

I nod.

She scribbles something down. "Describe this last one for me."

I sigh, annoyed, and then shake my head. I don't want to relive it. "It's the same as all the others," I reply.

"You're trapped in the car," she begins saying. "The fire."

I nod. I know it's impossible, but when she mentions the word fire, it feels like hot flames suddenly attack my skin. Images of that paparazzi guy filming me, as I begged for help, trapped inside the burning inferno of my car, flash instantly through my mind.

It's been a year since that horrific night, but it feels like it happened only yesterday.

After eight months of rehabilitation, I finally started walking again. I've had multiple operations – on my body and my face. I have scars everywhere. I still have a few more facial surgeries scheduled, and as a result, I wear a mask whenever company is around. It's a white mask that wraps around my head. *Trust me*, you wouldn't want to see me without it. I guarantee if you saw my face, you'd scream and run away. I still cringe whenever I take the mask off and stare at myself in the mirror. I look like I'm straight out of a horror movie. But I'm not wearing any special effects makeup to look scary. This is my real face. I look like the deranged monster in a film I starred in a few years ago... *The Monster Under the Stairs*. I'm the female version of that gruesome beast. The doctors insist the next round of plastic surgery will do wonders. But I'm not so sure.

One thing is certain: I'll never look the way I did before the accident.

"I don't think prescribing you more medication to help you sleep is the answer, Melody."

I shoot my therapist an annoyed look.

"Why is that?" I ask, unable to hide my frustration.

She crosses her legs and glances at the pad of paper resting on her lap. She lowers her glasses down the ridge of her nose. "Well, I think the nightmares are a sign that you need to start dealing with what happened. The accident happened a year ago. It's time you start taking steps to reclaim your life."

"Here we go again," I mumble under my breath. She doesn't have any idea what I'm going through. She doesn't know what it was like, after the crash, when I finally got discharged from the hospital and came home. She doesn't know how dark and lonely that experience was… and still is. She doesn't know that I took a bottle of pills to kill myself but last minute forced myself to puke them up.

She has no clue. But she acts like she does, which is really fuckin' annoying.

I'm hanging by a thread here. The least this motherfucking therapist can do is prescribe me something to help me sleep.

"I know you don't want to hear what I have to say," she says, clearing her throat. "But I think it's the only way you'll be able to move past what happened."

"Move past what happened?" I blurt. "Do you even know what it's like to have everything you ever wanted, everything you worked for, snatched away from you? And then to top it off, I've become a side show freak."

"You can still write music," she begins to say.

I hold up my hand, cutting her off. "Don't! I'll never be able to step out on stage looking the way I do."

"But aren't you going to have another procedure –"

"Yeah, to make me look a little less freakish," I acknowledge. "But not by much. My face is permanently ruined. In this industry, it's not the music that matters but the image. And I'm a horror show. So, Jeanie, don't even begin lecturing me on what you think I need to do. You have no idea what I'm going through. Just do your job and prescribe me more sleeping pills."

She looks at me shocked and slowly shakes her head. "No."

"Fuck you," I snap.

She sighs and takes off her glasses.

"At some point, Melody, you're going to have to make a choice. Right now, you're stuck in a moment, in a freeze frame. I'm not going to tell you I completely understand what you're going through. But I've counseled many patients who have suffered traumatic injuries. You have to begin with baby steps. For example, instead of insisting to meet in your house, we could have had this session in my office downtown."

I shake my head. "Hello? Have you not noticed the paparazzi in front of my house? They're dying to get me on camera. It's safer this way."

She motions with her arm to the room we're in. "So, is your plan to stay stuck here, in your mansion, for the rest of your life?" she asks.

I look at her and shrug. "Maybe. At least I know I'm safe here."

"Let's explore that more," she says leaning back in her chair. "So, you feel safe in your house. But the world outside makes you feel what?"

She stares at me, waiting for an answer. I fuckin' hate her. I am boiling over with frustration. I shoot her a dirty look through my mask. But I doubt she can see it.

"Are you going to prescribe me more sleeping pills, or what?"

She shakes her head. "I really think we need to address the underlining issue–"

"The underlining issue," I say cutting her off, "is that you're a shitty therapist and you're fired. I should have fired you years ago."

She looks surprised. I guess she didn't see that coming.

I point my finger at her and hiss. "Jeanie, I'm paying you a thousand dollars an hour because you're supposed to be some amazing therapist. But from what I can tell, you're an overpriced hack. And if you're not going to prescribe medicine to help me sleep, then what the fuck are you good for? I think it's time you get out of my house."

After a stunned silence, Dr. Jeanie Mendelsohn finally replies, "I see." Looking visibly flustered, she gets up from her chair and walks out of my study. I follow her out. As we walk the long hallway to my kitchen, and toward the back entrance of my house, she advises, "I think you need to start facing what's happened, Melody, and not run away from it. You need to accept that there are certain things you can not change."

"Well, the one thing I can change," I respond, "is therapists." When we enter the kitchen, I open the door leading into my backyard. I don't use the front door of my house anymore. I don't want those paparazzi assholes surrounding the front gate to get video of me. As I fling the backdoor open, I'm surprised to see Suzie standing outside. She has her set of keys in her hand.

"Hey, Melody." She then notices Dr. Mendelsohn standing next to me. "Hi Jeanie."

"She's leaving," I say sharply. "For good."

Dr. Mendelsohn walks past me; her face is red and angry. I motion Suzie to come inside. Once she's in the house, I close the door on Jeannie.

"You need to find me another therapist," I tell Suzie flatly as I walk toward the kitchen counter island.

"Seriously?" she replies. "I thought you liked her?"

"She's a hack. Remember when she thought I had a sex addiction problem?"

"Well, I kind-a-thought you had one too, " Suzie admits.

"Really?"

Suzie shrugs. "Just a little one, not a full blown addiction. But face it, Melody, you had a hard time keeping your legs together."

"I haven't had sex in a year!" I shout. "I do not have a sex addiction problem!"

"Before the accident, it was debatable," Suzie replies.

"Whatever," I grumble. "Just find me a therapist who actually knows what he or she is talking about, okay?"

"I'll see what I can do." She places a bunch of letters on the counter.

"What's that?" I ask.

"Fan mail."

"Seriously?"

Suzie nods.

"Haven't they heard of email?" I ask.

Suzie rolls her eyes. "Melody, you haven't replied to fan emails since the accident. You're not on social media anymore. Some of your loyal fans really want to hear from you. They want to know how you're doing. I think it's cool that some of them actually took the time to write you a real, physical letter."

I stare at the stack of envelopes resting on the counter.

"Can you reply for me?" I ask.

"No," she says, shaking her head. "That's bad karma.

Plus, I think it would be good for you to start writing again, even if it's only letters."

Suzie is the only one who can tell me what to do. Maybe because she's my lifeline to the outside world. Since the accident, she takes care of everything for me. She's the only person I trust.

"I've got a plumber coming by tomorrow to take a look at the toilet upstairs," Suzie says as she studies the calendar on her phone.

I look at her with worry. I don't like to interact with strangers. I don't like them staring at me. "You're going to be here to deal with him, right?"

Suzie nods. "Yes, I'll be here. I'm just reminding you. And don't forget we have an appointment with Dr. Henry this Wednesday. It's a consultation before the next plastic surgery."

I sigh as I take a seat on one of the stools surrounding the kitchen island.

"I'm sick of doctors," I mutter.

"Well, you only have two more procedures to go," Suzie says, her tone always positive. "Pretty soon you'll be able to take off that mask."

The thought of exposing myself to others frightens me to death. Once the plastic surgery is done, I'm still not sure I'll be able to take off this mask. My face is always going to look weird, scarred.

"I'm going to the store now," Suzie says. "Is there anything else you need that's not on the list?"

"Oreo Cookies," I reply.

"Got it." Suzie adds it to the list on her phone. "Now, remember, tonight I've got a date. So, I can't come over for movie night."

I nod. Every Monday night, Suzie comes over to watch a movie with me. I've lost touch with everyone else in my life since the accident.

"Okay, hon, I gotta go." Suzie gives me a hug before she leaves.

The door closes behind her. Then I turn toward the stack of letters. I sigh as I remove my mask and place it on the kitchen counter. I reach for one of the letters. I'm about to open it, when suddenly, I stop. These letters are addressed to Melody Swanson.

She no longer exists. She's dead.

I raise my hand and gently touch the patchwork of skin on my face. I can't go back to being the person I was, the person these fans remember. I don't know who I am anymore. But I'm definitely not her.

I'm nobody. I'm just a freak.

If I read these letters, I'll be reminded of everything I've lost. I place the letter on the counter and walk out of the kitchen.

It's 9 pm. I'm about to sit on my living room couch to watch a movie, when I decide to grab a bottle of wine from the kitchen. I notice the stack of letters still resting on the counter where Suzie left them this morning. I know Suzie won't stop bugging me until I reply to some of them.

Damn it! She's such a pain.

Although I know I'm going to regret it, I grab a bottle

of pinot grigio from the refrigerator and sit at my kitchen counter. I snatch one of the letters from the pile and quickly open it. The letter is from a young girl named Jessica Alvarez. She's sixteen and lives in Eugene, Oregon. She says she misses me and describes how important my music has been in her life. She hopes I'm doing okay since the accident. She writes that she hopes to hear my new album soon and see me on tour again.

I open a few more letters. Many of them echo the same sentiment. People miss me, hope I'm doing well, and can't wait to see me on tour and hear my new music.

I don't know what to write back. I'm at a loss for words. I glance at the remaining pile of unopened letters. I can't keep doing this. These people have expectations that I just can't meet anymore. Too much has changed. I'm no longer Melody Swanson. Don't they understand? I'm just a jumbled body of deformed skin. I have nothing to sing about and no desire to ever perform again.

The bitterness overwhelms me, and I swipe the pile of letters to the floor. I pick up my bottle of wine and head back to the living room. In darkness, I sit on my sofa and drink straight from the bottle.

I can't go on like this anymore.

As I sip from the bottle, that scary thought creeps into my mind once more. Maybe I should try again? Kill myself. I just need the courage to follow through. I still have some pills left over from last time.

7

Melody

"I don't want a dog."

"Honey, he's adorable."

I stare at the puppy laying in my lap. He's a two-month old English bulldog, with a light brown coat and white spots. I look at my mom and dad. They flew in for a surprise visit. I've been avoiding talking to them for months.

The only way they managed to see me was by showing up at my gate this morning and ringing the intercom. I had no choice but to let them in, or they might have talked to the reporters camped outside. When I opened the back door, I was surprised to see my mom holding this puppy in her hands.

"They say dogs are therapeutic," my father advises.

"And a ton of work," I reply. "I can't deal with that right now."

My parents take a seat on the couch, on either side of me. My dad pats the bulldog and he begins to lick his fingers.

"Take him," I say, trying to hand the puppy to my father.

"No," he says shaking his head. "If you insist on staying locked up in this place, you should at least have some company."

"Your dad's right," my mom affirms. She stares at me through her crystal blue eyes. "You can't be alone forever."

I look down at the puppy. He's got a scrunched-up, wrinkly face and oversized paws. He looks at me with affection and places his front legs on my chest. Then he begins nudging my facemask with his short snout.

I freak out.

I quickly hand the puppy to my mother and stand up. I anxiously check that my mask is on properly.

"Are you okay, honey?" asks my father coming up behind me. He places a hand on my shoulder.

I quickly shrug it off.

"I think you should go," I say, turning around and facing him. I notice the stunned expression on both my parents' faces.

"We thought we could stay the weekend," replies my mother.

I shake my head. "Not going to happen."

My father steps forward. "Sweetie, we're really worried about you."

I laugh sarcastically through my mask.

I've been supporting both my parents since I was eighteen. When I originally started in the business, they were both my managers. But I fired them four years ago when I discovered they were stealing from me. My mom and dad had funneled over fifteen million dollars into an offshore account without my knowledge. When my accountant uncovered their scheme, he immediately called me. I told my parents that I never wanted to see them again. But they threatened to write a tell-all book about me. So, I agreed to keep them on the payroll on one condition: they had to sign a non-disclosure agreement that stipulates they will never talk to the media. The fact that they're telling me they're concerned about my well being is sort of a joke. They just want my career to continue so the money doesn't dry up. Loving, caring parents I do not have. They're a pair of sharks as far as I'm concerned… and I'm sick of it.

"You two don't give a shit about me," I snap. "You're two of the most selfish people I know. I'm your meal ticket, and you're afraid it might come to an end. But don't try to come off like you actually care about my well being. You never have! When I was getting sick during my first tour and suffering from exhaustion, who showed up with uppers for his daughter to take? You did, Dad!" Then, I point my finger at my mom. "And when the label said they needed me to lose some weight before they'd consider signing me, who showed up with diet pills and held my hair while I vomited into the toilet after lunch everyday? That's right. You did, Mom." I point my finger at both of them. "You two are the worst fuckin' parents a kid could ask for. But you won the lottery because your daughter can sing a tune. But those days are over. My signing days are done. That's it! Over! The money train has finally reached the end of the tracks. Now get the fuck out of my house."

Their faces turn pale white. They exchange shocked looks. My mother clears her throat. She places the puppy down and slowly gets up from the couch. She straightens her red skirt and then approaches me. Her face is cold, icy. "I gave birth to you, you ungrateful –"

"What do you want? A fuckin' medal for opening your legs."

She smacks me across the face. My mask slips off and I cringe at the stinging pain. I look up and see the stunned expression on my mom's face. I turn and see the same expression on my father. My face! They've seen my face and they're horrified! The look in their eyes says it all. I look like a monster.

"I'm sorry. I shouldn't have done that, Melody," says my mother, stepping forward, her voice shaking.

I scramble backward, away from her. I hurry to readjust my mask. When I sense it's back in place, I yell, "Get the fuck out! Now!"

My parents look at each other and finally decide it's time to go.

I lead them toward the kitchen in silence. I open the back door and raise my arm showing them the way out.

"I'm sorry, Melody. I shouldn't have done that," repeats my mom, her voice low, filled with regret.

"I never want to see you again," I hiss.

I slam the door in their faces.

Suddenly, I hear whimpering. I storm into the living room and see the puppy scrambling around on the couch.

"Shit," I mutter.

I scoop him up and run with him to the backdoor. I step outside and hurry toward the driveway. The gate is closing as my parents take off in their rental car. I notice some cameras peering through the slits in the gates.

"There she is!" I hear somebody shout. "It's Melody!"

The reporters outside my house go crazy. "Melody! Melody!" they scream hysterically. I glance over and see a guy dangling from a tree, pointing his camera at me.

Totally freaking out, I scramble out of view and hurry inside my house, cradling the puppy in my arms.

I slam the door behind me and lean against it, trying to catch my breath.

The puppy huffs in my arms and begins licking my hand. I look down at him and sigh.

"Now I'm stuck with you," I complain.

8

Melody

"What are you going to name him?"

"I'm not. I want Randy to take him when she leaves."

"But he might help you; like your dad said, as a form of therapy."

I shoot Suzie a look. She shrugs in response. "I'm just saying. Anyways, he's so cute. Look at that mug. You have to keep him."

I look down at the puppy resting in my lap.

"So, it's settled; you're keeping the dog," says my agent, Randy, as she takes a seat on the chaise opposite me. "Now, it's time we talk business."

I look at Randy in disbelief. "Nothing's settled. I'm not keeping the dog."

"Melody, you haven't written a song in over a year," my agent replies. "Your dad may be a motherfucker, in more ways than one. But he does have a point: dogs are proven to be therapeutic." She crosses her long legs and stares at me.

"I don't want a dog," I whine.

Suzie steps forward and takes the puppy from me, holding him close to her face. "You're so cute. How could anyone not want you?"

The bulldog licks Suzie's face and she giggles.

"I have an idea," I say. "Suzie, why don't you keep him?"

"He's so adorable," she replies as she scratches the puppy behind the ears. Then Suzie's face turns serious, like she's realized something. She looks at me and shakes her head. "Nope. Randy and your dad are right. Dogs are therapeutic. You need this puppy, Melody. All you've been doing for months is moping around this house. This cutie pie is just what you need to get out of your funk. He'll help you get out of your head."

She hands the puppy back to me.

I stare at the puppy's wrinkly face and then look at both of them. "A dog is not going to help me write a song."

"Then what will?" asks Randy. "I know you're not done with all of your treatments. But we should get things in place for when you're ready to face the world again. The label said they're still behind you a hundred percent. They want to go all out with the next album. Pull out all the stops." She takes a breath and shrugs. "How about this; keep the dog for a week. If you don't write a song during that time, then Suzie can take him."

"There's not going to be a next album," I protest. "I'm not performing live ever again."

I get up from the sofa and hand Suzie the puppy. I walk toward the bay window looking out on my backyard. I notice my reflection in the window, the white mask covering my face. I look like the Phantom of the Opera.

"I'm not going to let them promote me like some kind of freak," I mutter.

"They're not going to promote you like a freak," responds Randy. "The whole world wants to hear your next album. This accident has only brought you closer to your fans. Don't you understand that, Melody?"

I scoff. "Closer to my fans? Once they take a look at me, they're going to run for the hills."

"Stop it," says Randy, getting up from the chaise and joining me by the window. "Melody, you're going to have to face them sooner or later. Or do you plan on staying locked up in your mansion for the rest of your life and have Suzie do everything for you?"

"Sounds like a plan to me," I reply. "Suzie, you don't mind, do you?"

Suzie, who's still holding the puppy, looks down, and shakes her head.

"Come on, that's not being realistic, Melody." Randy places her hand on my shoulder. "After a few more rounds of plastic surgery, you're going to look brand new. And when your fans hear your new songs, you're going to pick up right where you left off. You can put this whole nightmare behind you."

I shoot Randy a look of disbelief.

"Randy, you make it sound so easy."

"I know it's not going to be easy," she replies.

"No one says it's going to be easy," chimes in Suzie.

I stare at both of them. They just don't get it. "The doctor said no matter how many operations, there's still going to be scarring," I tell them. "The only difference is that I'll look a little less hideous than I do right now. Do you want me to take off this mask? Because trust me, if you saw what I *really* looked like, you'd both turn away in disgust. You should have seen my parents' faces when they saw me without the mask. They were horrified."

"Maybe you're making it seem worse than it really is. You're being too critical," says Randy.

I feel a knot of anger growing inside me. I just want to be left alone. I don't want anyone telling me what I should do, or that I'm overreacting. They don't understand what I'm going through.

"Melody, I'm just –" begins Randy.

"Trying to get your ten percent," I snap, cutting her off.

Randy looks at me, shocked. The floodgates of rage have opened, and I'm far from finished. "You and I both know a new album and tour will make money. Why? Because everybody loves the scene of an accident. And that's what I am: a human car crash. I can see it now. My nasty face plastered all over the entertainment news. Sure, I'll get some sympathy media coverage for a while; but then it will stop. Why? Because nobody likes to look at a freak for too long. We just want what's beautiful. I could have the voice of an angel and the talent of the gods. But if I'm ugly, nobody buys tickets. We'd rather swim in a sea of mediocrity as long as it looks attractive. You and I both know, Randy, that ugly people never make it in this business. And I'm hideous now. You're just hoping I knock out this last album and do one last tour so you can squeeze whatever your ten percent is worth. Then you'll quit being my agent. Which is fine, because my career is over anyway."

Randy looks visibly hurt. "How can you say that about me, Melody?"

"I just did."

Randy looks at the floor, at a loss for words. She takes a deep breath and raises her hands. "I'm going to give you the benefit of the doubt here, Melody, because you and I go way back, to the beginning when you were performing in coffee shops, remember? You slept on my couch countless times because your mom and dad were being total assholes." She closes her eyes and takes another breath. "Maybe you need some time to cool off, and then we can talk."

"I don't have anything else to say. I'm not writing any more songs or touring. I'm finished. Look at me, Randy! All the music I had inside me died in that car crash. I'm just an empty shell now."

"You're twenty-five years old, Melody. You have your whole life –"

"My life is over!" I shriek.

Silence.

Randy and Suzie exchange glances.

Then Randy looks at me and says softly, "This is the next chapter of your life, Melody. We never saw this coming, but it's not the end. Suzie and I have your back, no matter what." She pauses, and then says, "But I have to tell you something, and you're not going to like it. But you need to understand the repercussions of your decision."

"What?"

Randy sighs. "If you don't produce another album, the label can go after you for breach of contract."

"What are you talking about?"

"When we signed with the label years ago, the contract stipulated that you are legally obligated to produce five albums for them. If they don't get that last album, they can take you to court and sue. They can go after all your assets." She looks around. "Even this house."

"They can't do that," I protest.

"Legally, they can," says Randy.

"Why did we sign that?"

Randy shrugs. "It was industry standard at the time. And, remember, your mom and dad were calling a lot of the shots for you back then."

I can't believe this is happening.

"Fuck," I grumble and look at the ground.

Randy looks at me with concern. "Melody, I've been trying to get you to write music since the accident because I think it will help you through this tough time. But that's not the only reason. You have a gift that the world needs to hear. But the sad truth is, even if you aren't ready to write any songs, the label can legally force you too. They can make your life a living hell. And after everything you've been through, that's the last thing any of us want."

Randy places her hand on my shoulder. "I'm sorry it's come to this," she says.

Randy leaves shortly thereafter. Once she's gone, I slowly turn around. Suzie is staring at me, still holding the puppy in her hands.

"What are you going to do?" she asks.

An idea takes shape in my mind. "I'll just write some crappy music and send it to them," I reply. "Randy never mentioned the songs needed to be any good."

Suzie shakes her head and sighs. She walks toward me and tries to hand over the puppy, but I won't take him.

"Well, if that's your plan," she says. "I won't be working for you anymore. I'm still your friend, Melody, but no longer your personal assistant."

I can't believe what she just said. "What? You can't be serious?"

Suzie nods. "Melody, I begged to be your assistant five years ago because I love your music. And Randy is right; you have a real gift that you need to share with the world. But if you're just going to quit and write crap to get out of some contract, I don't want to be around to witness it. I love you too much and it will be too painful to watch."

She turns and walks out of the living room, carrying the puppy. I quickly follow her. I realize I can't lose Suzie. She's my only connection to the outside world. She does everything for me: shopping, dry-cleaning, meeting with people, etc… And not only that, she's my best friend, my only *real* human connection. She visits me every day!

"I'll triple your salary," I blurt in desperation.

Suzie turns around. "This isn't about money, Melody. You know that."

"You can't leave me. *I need you*. I can't go out there."

The thought of losing Suzie is bringing on a panic attack. I can feel the swell of anxiety. Suzie must sense the turmoil I'm experiencing, because she looks at me concerned. Then a curious expression crosses her face. "I'll stay on one condition."

"Anything," I beg. Thank goodness. A sense of relief comes over me.

"You write a song," she says.

Damn it! I throw my head back, annoyed. "Come on."

"I'm being serious," says Suzie. "You write a song by Wednesday and I'll stay on as your personal assistant for another month."

"How about I quadruple your salary instead?" I plead.

But Suzie isn't interested.

"I'm not talking about an entire album, Melody. Just one song. And not a song for the masses. A song for you. A song conveying the emotions crammed inside you. And I get to hear it. Do we have a deal?"

I look at the floor, hesitating. I can't lose Suzie. She's all I've got, my only friend and confidant. I look up at her. "One song and you'll stay my assistant and still come by everyday?"

Suzie nods.

She has me cornered.

"Fine. I'll do it."

Suzie's face breaks out in a smile. "Awesome!" She hurries forward and hands me the puppy. It tumbles into my arms. "I love you," she says and quickly kisses the forehead part of my mask. "I'll stop by tomorrow morning. Now listen, there's dog food on the counter. I brought some over when you told me about the dog. I've got to run. I'm late for my Pilates class."

Before I know what's happening, she closes the door behind her. I look down at the puppy in my hands.

"I just can't get rid of you," I say.

The little bulldog begins licking my hand again.

9

Melody

I'm back in the car, engulfed by flames. My skin sizzles from the heat. My eyes search frantically for an escape. My hands and shirt are covered in blood. "Help!" I shout at the top of my lungs. There's smoke everywhere. I'm coughing, struggling to fill my lungs with air. Part of the car door is jabbed into my side, puncturing my flesh. "Help!" I feel something sharp piercing my face, but I can't move to relieve the pressure. "Help!" A bright light beams through my broken windshield.

Then I see him, fuckin' Charlie: his beard, his camera lens. He's filming this!

"Help!" I scream, but he just keeps pointing his camera as the flames engulf me. The pain is unbearable. I hear cars honking in the distance, then the loud siren of an ambulance. The flames grow. The scent of burning flesh filters through my nostrils.

Startled, I shoot up in bed, screaming.

I quickly run my hands over my arms. I am fine, still scarred, but NOT on fire. I immediately touch my face. I feel the stretched, ragged skin. I sigh, relieved. It was just another nightmare – a flashback to that horrific night.

Then I hear a loud, high-pitched yelp.

It's that darn puppy.

So much for an afternoon nap.

I get out of bed and drag my feet to the door. When I open it, the puppy energetically shuffles in and begins circling my feet. I bend down and scoop him up. He happily licks my face. I'm not wearing my mask. But I realize it doesn't really matter. This little guy doesn't seem to care what I look like. He runs his wet tongue all over my exposed nose and cheek.

"Okay, enough, buddy," I giggle.

He stretches so he can continue licking my face. I hold him back. He huffs.

"What? Do you have a thing for ugly girls?" I ask him.

He barks a reply and looks at me with his playful puppy eyes.

"Damn, you are cute," I mutter as I take in his scrunched up, wrinkly mug.

He huffs again, like he knows he's cute.

Holding him, I turn back to the bed and cringe, remembering the nightmare I just had. Every time I try to sleep, that nightmare waits for me, ready to wreak havoc. I sigh and walk out of the bedroom, carrying the little English bulldog in my arms.

I was hoping an afternoon nap would put me in a better disposition to write a song. No such luck.

As I venture into the living room, still carrying the puppy, I see the grand piano situated in the corner. When writing a song, I like to compose something on the piano before I take it into my home recording studio and add additional musical layers. It's just how I like to work. I haven't touched the piano since the accident. I haven't ventured into my home recording studio down the hall in just as long.

As I stare at the imposing black frame of the piano, I begin to shudder. I don't know if I can do this: write a song that's actually good. It's been so long.

The puppy whimpers.

I look at him.

"I know. But if I don't write something decent, Suzie will leave us."

The puppy whimpers again.

I nod. "I know. I love her. But what a bitch, right?"

I walk over to the piano bench. I'm wracked with tension. It's so strange. I used to sit at this piano every morning. It was part of my daily ritual. I actually used to look forward to it. But now, I'm a nervous wreck as I contemplate sitting down to compose.

The puppy huffs repeatedly.

"Okay. Okay."

I plop down on the piano bench.

My hands shake as I slowly lift the fallboard covering the keys. I stare at the ebony and ivory and that rush of anxiety comes back. I really, really don't know if I can do this.

I don't think I have any music left in me. I'm a void.

The puppy whimpers again and licks my fingers with his wet tongue.

I nod. "You're right. Suzie's such a bitch for putting me through this. Blackmailing me to write a song is so not cool."

I place the puppy on the floor. Then I take a deep

breath and cautiously place my trembling fingers on the keys.

10

Melody

Two vodka sodas, one fat joint, and I still have nothing. No verse, no chorus. Nothing that isn't cringe worthy. I look down at the puppy resting beside me on the piano bench.

He stuck by me through this entire miserable process.

I hand him another dog biscuit. He munches on it greedily. When he's finished, I pick him up and hold him close to my face. He begins licking it all over again, lathering up the scar tissue. I guess he doesn't see the defects. "You're the only one," I mutter as I lower him to my lap.

He meets my gaze with his warm, innocent puppy eyes.

"I've got a name for you," I declare as I stare at his sad looking mug. "Mingus. Don't ask me why," I shrug. "It's just what popped into my head right now."

Mingus licks my fingers. I guess he approves.

"Okay, enough of that," I say. "I have to get back to work. Suzie says she doesn't want a crappy song, so here we go again…"

I lower Mingus to the floor and place my hands back

on the piano keys. I begin searching for a tune. But after an hour of chasing dead ends, I'm right back where I started... nowhere. Suzie wants something real from me, not some pop dribble that doesn't say anything. A song about singing in the shower or taking a selfie won't cut it. Not that I could ever write that kind of crap anyway. But the truth is, I feel so blocked, so rigid, that nothing's coming to the surface. I have a million emotions swirling inside of me – everything from grief to anger – but I can't translate any of it to the keys, or put it into verse.

I'm frustrated beyond belief.

And after my third vodka soda... I'm also, really, really horny.

I laugh sarcastically. A year ago, my therapist thought I couldn't go a month without sex.

"Told you I didn't have a problem," I mumble. I'm closing in on dry month number thirteen. I take another sip from my drink.

Flashbacks to all the crazy sex I had – in my short but eventful life – slowly play through my mind. Each one makes me hotter... and hornier.

I've masturbated plenty of times during my self-imposed lockdown. But I've grown tired of my hand and my toys. What I desperately long for is a man's hard body, writhing against mine. His hard cock sliding between my legs and filling me with its girth.

Then I notice my reflection off the piano's shiny black wood.

I sigh.

I realize something, as I stare at my scarred, damaged face.

I'm totally unfuckable.

Any idea you have after four vodka sodas is usually a bad one. But after fiddling with my piano for another hour, and reminiscing about the hot sex I used to have, I just couldn't take it anymore. No man, of his own free will, would ever want to sleep with me. But I have over thirty million dollars in the bank. I'm sure I can find someone I can *pay* to do the deed.

I decide to go online. I begin searching site after site. I've never done anything like this before – actively searched databases for someone to fuck me. Before the accident, I had men lining up to pleasure me. I was a catch. But now, post accident, I'll need money to entice someone to fuck me.

It astounds me how many sites are dedicated to selling sex, in one form or the other. With so much to choose from, it becomes a bit overwhelming.

You can have any flavor you want, in any combination.

I begin clicking from one site to another. So many men to choose from… but none of them are jumping off the page.

Sure, a lot of these guys are good looking, but in a plastic kind of way. They're all exquisitely tanned and groomed. And their bodies, although muscular, look too sculpted, too steroid ridden.

I'm not looking for a model; or one of those guys who spends all day at the gym, obsessing about his body mass index. I'm looking for a real man. Someone who can fuck me the way I need to be fucked. Someone whose got an edge, some fire. Someone I can sense is simmering underneath the surface.

I click to another site.

It's a website dedicated to military men: veterans who are now selling their bodies for cash. I click from one profile to another…

Then I stop.

Those eyes.

They're dark, intense, resentful… haunted.

They reflect exactly how I feel. I read his profile. He's done two tours in Iraq, one in Afghanistan. He's a mixed martial arts fighter. As I stare at his face, and his dark haunted eyes, I can tell this dude has seen some shit. There's something devastating underneath his hard look. I can feel it. It draws me in.

I'm practically drooling at the sight of his body. He's rock solid, heavily tattooed. And upon closer examination, I even notice some scars – probably from the battlefield. This guy is the *real* man I've been looking for. He's also hot as fuck. But it's his eyes that draw me to him. I can't explain it, but I feel a connection to him, even though he's just a picture on a website.

I sound foolish, but it's true.

I have another sip from my drink. Can I really go through with this? Call a complete stranger to have sex with me? It's been so long since I've had anyone touch me in a sensual way. I wonder if my body even knows how to respond. But then again, maybe a sexual encounter is *exactly* what I need to start feeling like a human being. After all, sex was such a big part of my life before the accident.

I take a deep breath and decide to go for it.

Mingus, who is resting on my lap, huffs. I look at him.

"Hey, don't judge me, Mingus. I need to deliver a song to Suzie by Wednesday. I can't help it if sex may be the only way I get inspired."

Mingus lowers his head, acquiescing to my logical drunken argument.

I take another sip from my drink. Then I take a deep breath and click the link below his picture. Another window pops up, alerting me that a call is being placed to my "friend."

I take another sip from my vodka as it continues ringing.

When the ringing stops, I hear his voice. It's low, baritone and steady.

"Hello. This is Kade."

I find myself struggling to speak.

11

KADE

It's dark. I can't see anything. I walk down the hallway of a dilapidated building. Gunfire and screams ring in my ears. I'm wearing my combat uniform. Am I back in the Middle East? The building I walk through appears to be a rundown hospital. As I make my way down the hall, the smell of gunpowder filters through the air. I clench the rifle in my hands. The human screams continue, and slowly, one of them becomes more predominant.

Soon, it's the only cry I hear.

It's Max.

"Daddy! Daddy!" He's crying for help. I race down the hall, clutching my gun, searching room after room.

I finally find him. He's in one of the rooms, standing by an open window. There's an angel – with white wings surrounded by a blinding white light – standing next to him.

"Max, get away from her!" I shout.

Max turns to me with a smile and says, "It's okay, Dad. I'm going with my new friend."

"Don't leave!" I shout.

"It's okay, Dad," Max repeats.

"No, it's not," I mutter, tears streaming down my face.

The angel motions Max to follow her through the open window.

"Bye, Daddy," says Max with one last wave. "I love you."

The blinding white light fills the room. When the light subsides, I'm standing alone, tears still streaming down my face. Then I notice blood pouring from my chest.

I've been shot in the heart.

I wake up frantically. My cellphone is ringing. My face is wet. Fuck, was I crying in my sleep? I wipe my eyes and reach for the nightstand. I glance at the time stamp on my phone: 2:00 a.m.. Then I notice the number. It's a call from the website. If I don't pick up, Shane will know. He monitors everything on the site. I sigh and answer.

"Hello. This is Kade."

Silence.

"Hello?" I repeat. "Anybody there?"

I'm annoyed. If you're going to call me at 2 a.m., you better have something to say.

Then, she finally speaks.

"Hi…I…uh…I'm sorry, did I wake you?"

I rub my eyes. I decide to be honest.

"Yeah. It's all right though. I was having a nightmare."

"Oh," she says. There's a long pause. Then she finally speaks. "I'm sorry… I don't… I think I've made a mistake."

Like I said, Shane has someone monitoring the site.

And he hasn't been too pleased with the number of customers I've booked this month. I owe him a ton of money. And with my lackluster sales rate, it's going to take me *two* lifetimes to pay him back. I have to keep this girl talking and *hopefully* have it lead to an actual meeting.

"How can you be so sure?" I blurt. "We haven't even talked yet."

Another long silence. I can hear her breathing.

"I've never done this before?" she admits.

"Called somebody at two a.m.?" I say, trying to be light hearted. It doesn't come naturally to me, but Shane says I need to get better at it so clients feel at ease.

"You know what I mean," she replies. "I've never used a website for this sort of thing."

I sit up in bed. I have to keep her on the phone.

"I really think I've made a mistake," she repeats.

"The only mistake you'll be making is hanging up," I quickly say. My words disgust me. I take a deep breath and decide to speak honestly. I've never been good at faking it… ever. "Listen. I know this might be something out of the ordinary for you. But you've called for a reason. You need something. There's something missing from your life. Am I right?"

Another long pause.

"I miss being with a man," she admits. She takes a breath and continues. "I'm lonely. I've been lonely for a long time."

"Most people are," I tell her. *I know I am.*

"I guess that's good for your business," she replies, a little sarcastically.

"What do you miss about being with a man?" I ask.

"What do you mean? Like specifics?"

"Yeah," I reply. "It will help me get a better sense of whether I can help you."

She takes a moment.

"Let me see… everything," she says with a sigh. "I miss everything about a man: his hands running over my skin, his breath against my neck, the muscles in his arms, his smell, his masculine energy, and definitely his cock."

As she talks, I realize how amazing her voice sounds. It's rich, sensual, layered. It sneaks into you, warms you. As she describes what she likes, I find myself getting surprisingly turned on. It's her voice: it's captivating. I wonder what this woman looks like.

"Why'd you choose me?" I ask, when she finishes.

She takes another long pause. "Something in your eyes. They lured me in."

"I've never had anyone mention my eyes before," I confess. "Usually they notice the tattoos. What about my eyes?" I ask, trying to keep the conversation flowing. After all, this lady is getting billed every thirty seconds.

Another long pause. Then she finally speaks, her voice low, like a whisper. "They're haunted."

Her words linger in the air.

"Haunted?" I repeat.

"Yeah," she replies.

Suddenly, I'm knocked out of the moment. This doesn't feel like my standard website call. There's something more going on here. The emotion in this woman's voice, the fact she says my eyes are haunted… This isn't just a hire-a-fuck call.

"My eyes are haunted. That's what you like about

them, huh?"

I wait for her response. She finally admits, "When I saw them, I just felt like you might be able to relate to me."

Now it's my turn to be quiet. I don't know how to respond. Who's this stranger that's just called me in the middle of the night? First, she says I'm haunted. Then, she thinks she can relate to me. How would she know?

"I hope I haven't offended you," she says when I don't say anything.

"No," I tell her. "You just caught me off guard. I guess haunted is an accurate description of me these days."

I hear her sigh. "Me too," she admits quietly. Then her tone changes, her voice grows stronger. "I think I'm building up the courage to go through with this," she says. "Can we meet?"

I'm still thrown off by our exchange and take a moment to respond. "Yeah, of course. Tonight?"

"Yes. Is that a problem?"

"Not at all," I say. "I promise; you won't be disappointed." I hate saying that line but Shane insists.

"Satisfaction guaranteed, huh?" She replies. Damn her voice sounds sexy. It's sarcastic and feminine but with many layers to it. It's full bodied like a fine wine.

"Before we meet," I tell her. "I need to ask you something."

"Okay," she replies.

"You're not a cop, are you?"

She laughs. "No."

"Good. I just needed to check. Well, now that that is

settled, why don't we discuss some details."

She says she's just interested in a quick session. She doesn't know what she wants, and we decide to figure it out when we meet. When I mention my fee, she doesn't hesitate and says it won't be a problem. I ask her where she wants to meet and she says her home. I find that a bit unusual since I meet most of my clients in hotels.

"How long will it take you to get here?" she asks.

"Well, you have to tell me where you live first."

"Duh. Sorry."

She gives me her address. It's all the way on the other side of town… in the Hollywood hills, celebrity central. A far cry from my ghetto neighborhood in South LA.

"It's the middle of the night, so not long," I tell her. "But you know LA. You never know when you're going to hit traffic."

"Can you leave now?" she asks. Now that she's made up her mind to go through with it, she doesn't want to waste any time.

"Sure."

"Great. See you soon."

She hangs up. I look at my phone, still surprised by the tone of our conversation.

Haunted.

I stretch my arms and slowly get out of bed. I'm back on the clock.

I step into the tiny bathroom of my shitty studio apartment and wash my face to wake up. As I dry off, I see the picture of Max pinned to the bathroom mirror. He's smiling back at me. The picture was taken when he was healthy… before the cancer. I kiss my lips and touch his picture.

"Tigers need their rest, son."

I turn off the bathroom light and walk out.

Tomorrow will be the nine-month anniversary of his death.

12

KADE

Fortunately, there isn't much traffic on the 110. So, I can probably make it up to the Hills in forty-five minutes. I roll down the window of my piece-of-shit Corolla and let the night breeze blow in. It's unusually hot in LA for February.

Fuckin' climate change.

I listen to some hip-hop to divert my mind. But that doesn't work. I turn off the radio.

As usual, I think about Max.

Tomorrow will mark nine months since I buried my son.

It all happened so fast.

After Shane offered to pay Max's medical bills, I immediately told the doctor to enroll him in the experimental procedure. We flew Max to Denver, Colorado for his treatment – that's where the premier doctor that dealt with Max's rare illness worked. Max and I spent two months there. At first, it looked like he was responding well to the treatment. But then suddenly, things took a turn for the worse.

I'm still amazed by how tough my son was until the

end.

I miss him so much. He was such a good kid. He didn't deserve to go through what he did. My heart bleeds every time I think of him. It's a pain – an emotion – I can't put into words.

Suddenly, I stop thinking about Max when – to my right – about a mile ahead, I notice a car pulled over on the highway. Instantly, the muscles in my neck tense. I grip the steering wheel for dear life. My heart races.

Here we go again.

My fight or flight responses kick into high alert. Is that car a decoy? Could it contain an explosive device – just like the car in Iraq that blew up my Humvee and killed two of my men. I was lucky; I escaped with only a few bruises.

A cold sweat pours down my face, as I get closer to the car parked on the shoulder. My instinct is to find an alternate route, a way out. My eyes swiftly scan the rearview mirror, then the side mirrors. I'm blocked by another car to my left. I can't stop, or swerve into another lane.

I'm getting closer.

I imagine the car exploding.

I ease off the accelerator, wanting to avoid passing the car altogether. The car behind me honks me out of my daze.

I have no way out of this. I have to drive past this car.

It's getting closer.

I grip the steering wheel so tight that I'm afraid it might snap off.

I'm about to pass it.

I tightly shut my eyes and wait for the explosion.

Suddenly, the car to my left honks. I open my eyes wide.

Shit! I'm about to hit the car!

I swerve back into my lane. I quickly look in my rear view mirror. The car on the shoulder is now a safe distance away. It looks like it had a flat tire.

I try reminding myself I'm not in Iraq or Afghanistan. I'm in LA. But my body can't tell the difference. It's on high alert now and I feel a sense of rage flood through me. I bang my steering wheel with frustration. Fuck this PTSD.

I take several deep breaths but it does nothing to calm me.

I'm so angry. Angry at a million different things all at once. I'm angry at the war and what it did to me. I'm angry at God for putting my son through so much pain and then robbing him of his life at such a young age.

I was the one who went to war. I should be the dead one, not my little boy.

I'm angry at life itself and how unfair it can be to some.

Then, a sense of guilt overwhelms me.

My anger slowly turns to regret.

I was a terrible father.

I should have spent more time with Max when he was alive.

Monique got pregnant right before I was shipped out on my first tour of Iraq. We were never a couple. We just had sex after a party one night and she got pregnant.

I was in the Middle East when Max was born. And

when I came home between tours, I wasn't very involved in either one of their lives. Honestly, I was a bit of a zombie. Acclimating to civilian life was really difficult for me. That's why I always went back to the Middle East. That all changed when I realized Monique was in really bad shape because of her drug habit. When I saw my son being raised in that environment, I realized I needed to do something. I finally took on my responsibilities as a father and put my combat days behind me. Max moved in with me. Monique disappeared. I still don't know where she went. I hope she's alive and hasn't died from drug abuse.

Max and I had a few happy years together, just the two of us. I channeled my PTSD anger issues into MMA fighting. But when the traveling became too much, I decided to open my own gym to spend more time with Max. Everything felt like it was finally falling into place.

I was finding joy in being a father.

Then Max got sick.

When I buried my son, my life fell apart. I lost everything.

Max's medical bills amounted to several hundred thousand dollars. Shane paid every one of them, on one condition: He owned me until the debt was repaid.

He owns my gym, and I have to fight in underground matches he promotes. He keeps all the earnings; I don't see a dime. But that's not where it ends.

He also owns my body.

Shane pimps me out through his website. Apparently, there's a huge demand among rich LA women for former military men who are built like me. So, when I'm not training for the next fight, I'm on the clock fucking.

I'm a whore. And Shane is my pimp.

This was the deal I made with him in exchange for paying Max's medical bills. To Shane, this is purely a business transaction. He needs to make back the money he loaned me. And the only thing I have of value is my gym and my body. In his view, this isn't personal. It's just business.

I don't know how much more of this I can take though. I've grown so numb to people, my surroundings…

I've come close to killing myself on more than one occasion. I keep a handgun in the drawer of my nightstand. On two separate nights, I've placed the muzzle of that gun in my mouth and tried to pull the trigger. But both times, the realization that I'd be letting my son, Max, down stopped me from going through with it. I believe Max is in heaven looking down at me. And I know he'd be really disappointed in his father if he quit on life.

But I'll be honest, it's getting harder for me to justify living in such a senseless world. What do I have to live for, anyway? I still have Layla, but I avoid seeing her and her family as much as possible. I just feel like my sad presence brings everyone down. I see the sadness in their eyes when I show up to their house and it reminds me of everything I've lost.

I force myself to stop thinking about all this as I take the next exit off the freeway. I'm about to meet a client. I have to get in the mood to fuck. As I weave my beat up Corolla through the curvy Hollywood hills, I glance at the mansions lining the street. So this is how the other half live – in a world where money is never a concern, and the future is always bright from inside your hilltop mansion. Must be nice.

The GPS tells me I've arrived at the address. I park my car.

I still don't know if I can go through with this tonight. I'm in such a sad, miserable state. But if I don't, I'll have to provide Shane an explanation. I don't feel like dealing with that either. I take a deep breath and get out of my car.

A full moon is shining in the night sky, casting shadows on the ground. I look at the modern mansion before me, overlooking LA. I make my way toward the gate. A red Volkswagen bug is parked down the street. It calls my attention because I can see the silhouette of someone inside the car. Looks like a guy with a beard. But it's dark, so I'm not sure.

I press the button on the intercom.

"Yes?"

"It's me. Kade."

"It took you long enough. I almost changed my mind."

"Well, you'll be glad you didn't," I respond. I hate talking like this. It's not me. But I remind myself that Shane wants me to be friendly and upbeat, not such a downer.

"Come around back. Don't use the front door," she says.

The gates open and I walk up the driveway toward the house. I ring the backdoor, as instructed. As I wait, I remember the reason this woman chose me from the website: my haunted eyes. Well, if haunted is what she's attracted to, she picked the right guy.

The door unlocks.

13

Melody

As I wait for him to knock on my door, I realize what I am doing. I'm letting a complete stranger into my house. What if he's a serial killer? Fuck, now I decide to worry about this? I've already let him through the gate and he's walking to my door! I quickly run to the safe in my bedroom and punch in the code. I unlock it and take out a small handgun. I've never fired it. I purchased it three years ago when I found a deranged-looking thirty-year-old man waiting for me in my kitchen with flowers. He broke into my house. He said his name was James, said he loved me, and wanted us to get married. I talked calmly to James as I texted 911 on my phone. James is now locked up in some psych ward.

My doorbell rings. I quickly slide open my nightstand drawer and place the gun inside. Now, it's easily accessible if anything crazy happens. I'm about to step out of the bedroom when I realize I don't have my mask on. I grab it and slip it on, then make sure it's tightly fastened behind my head so it won't slip. I check myself in the mirror. This white mask really makes me look like the Phantom of the Opera. I check my outfit. I'm wearing a long burgundy peasant skirt with a black tank top under a chambray shirt. For some strange reason, I hope this guy I'm paying to fuck me likes what I'm wearing. The doorbell rings again. I hurry out of the bedroom and toward the back door. Mingus runs after me the whole way. I realize he might be too much of a distraction, so I scoop him up and lock him in one of the bathrooms with a bowl of food and water.

"This is only temporary, Mingus. I just can't have you barking while I'm fucking. It's a mood killer."

Mingus whimpers a reply as I close the bathroom door. The doorbell rings again.

"I'm coming," I shout. I scurry toward the back door. I take a deep breath and touch my white plastic mask one last time – just to make sure it hasn't shifted. I don't want my scars to scare him away.

Finally, I open the door.

He's staring straight at me. Those dark, deep eyes set in a chiseled face. I scan his body.

Damn, he is fine.

He's wearing a tight black t-shirt and worn out blue jeans. It's a simple ensemble but one that highlights his perfect physique. This dude is rock solid: muscular, tattooed arms, strong thighs and legs. And his face: gorgeous – like it's been chiseled out of marble as some sculptor's idea of what the perfect man should look like. He has dark hair and full lips. But it's those damn eyes that really draw me in. They're so intense, brimming with emotion. Then I notice the surprised look on his face. It's my mask. I've caught him off guard. I didn't warn him beforehand. I touch the mask gently with my hand.

I'm about to comment on it but struggle with what to say.

So I say nothing.

We stare at each other in silence. I sense he's trying to figure out what kind of weird shit he signed up for. He gives me a slight nod and tries to smile, but I can tell it doesn't come naturally to him.

"Sorry, it took me a bit," he says. "I don't live anywhere near your neighborhood."

I hear the sadness in his voice. He's trying to hide it. But if you listen closely, you can sense it in the few words he just uttered.

It's been so long since I've had a man like this in my presence. Scratch that. I've never had a man as impressive as him stare at me before. And wearing this mask, I suddenly feel really foolish.

This was a mistake. But I've already opened the door. I have to let him in now. I take a deep breath and try to steady my nerves.

"Please come in," I say as I open the door wider so he can pass through.

I inhale as he walks past me. Damn... I've missed the scent of a man. And this guy, Kade, smells good, like the outdoors, woodsy but mixed with spice. I feel myself getting woozy from his presence. I convince myself it's because of him and not the vodka tonics I've had throughout the night.

He turns around and faces me, his hands in his jean pockets. He gives a quick glance around the place and shrugs.

"Nice place," he remarks, but I can tell by the way he

says it that he doesn't really care.

"Thanks."

We stand still, staring at each other again, saying nothing. Those eyes. I see an intense storm brewing in them. He's on the edge of something. Something deep and sorrowful. His energy might be dark and mysterious but it's also strangely comforting. My attraction toward him escalates. I can't explain why.

"I should have warned you," I say.

"About?"

"The mask."

He shrugs. "Whatever makes you comfortable is fine with me."

He keeps staring at me, and I realize if I'm going to go through with this, I should warn him about the scars on my body too.

"I had an accident," I say. "I have scars. All over my body. Including my face. I should have warned you over the phone." I take another deep breath. "If you want to cancel this meeting, I understand."

He ponders what I said, and I'm suddenly racked with nerves. I realize I don't want him to go. In the few seconds he's been in my home, I've felt the air shift around me. His dark, soulful presence is astonishing. It pulls me in, like the force of a magnet. And up close, he looks even hotter than his picture. Even though I'm nervous about it, I know I just have to see what he looks like underneath those clothes. I have to see him naked.

But I can't blame him if he doesn't want to have sex with my scar-covered body. I really should have mentioned it over the phone when I was talking to him.

Now it's awkward.

"Will it hurt? If I touch you?" he asks. I notice the concerned tone in his voice. I wasn't expecting it.

I shake my head. Then quickly make sure my mask hasn't shifted. "No," I say. "It won't hurt. But there are scars everywhere."

He shrugs. "I'm fine with it, if you are?" he says. "I just want to know if I need to be gentle."

Another long moment of silence. We keep staring at each other. His dark gaze is so intense. It's mesmerizing.

"Please don't be gentle," I confide. "I'm not that type of girl."

Did I just say that? I guess it's the vodka talking, but it's true.

Physical sex – the unbridled, no-holds barred kind – is what I prefer. Tonight will test whether my body can handle it after the accident.

"Good to know," he replies. After a pause, he admits with a shrug, "I'm not really the slow and romantic type."

Our eyes meet again and my body begins to tingle. It's been so long since I've felt the excited rush of sexual energy run through my veins.

"Do you want anything to drink?" I ask.

He shakes his head. "No thanks."

"Are you in training? Your profile said you're a fighter."

He nods. "Yeah. I fight underground."

"What makes it underground?"

"No rules."

"Sounds dangerous."

"Can be," he says with a shrug.

This Kade isn't much of a talker, but I don't care. I didn't hire him for that. I hired him to fuck me. And I get the impression he knows what he's doing in that department.

"Is this going to be your first time since the accident?" he asks.

I nod slowly.

"Well, I hope I can make it memorable," he says.

I smirk behind the mask. "Trust me, looking the way you do, I don't think it will be an issue."

I'm feeling bolder now, more comfortable. My attraction to this guy is growing with each passing second. And my sexual desire is coming back to life.

"Well, I'm here to please you," he says with another shrug, "Your satisfaction is guaranteed. If you don't like anything I do, just let me know." He pauses then says, "And if you want to take off that mask so you're comfortable –"

I raise my hand, cutting him off.

"You don't want to see what I look like underneath this thing." I touch the mask with my fingers. "You'd cringe, and it would ruin an already awkward encounter."

There's a pause, then he asks, "Why is this awkward?"

"Well, because of this mask," I confess.

He nods and looks at the ground. He's pondering what I just said. Then he looks at me. Staring straight into my eyes, he takes a few steps forward. I feel a nervous rush of excitement shoot through me. He begins to echo the words from our phone conversation. "I thought you called me because you wanted to get fucked. Wanted to feel my hands over your skin, my cock deep inside of you. Isn't that right?"

He moves in closer and my skin grows heated from his presence.

"That's right," I tell him.

He shrugs. "Well, that has nothing to do with how you look." He's even closer now. His voice turns into a whisper as he stares into me. "That's about our bodies colliding. The skin is just surface. Everything below it is what matters."

I inhale deeply; he's so close. "You smell good."

I'm hypnotized by his presence; by the way he looks at me. For a brief moment, he's made me feel like I'm not wearing a mask. I know he's probably putting on an act – his job is pleasuring people after all – but I appreciate what he just said. I'm happy with my decision. I've chosen the perfect man to have sex with since the accident. But before we go any further, I need to make sure of something.

"You won't tell anyone will you?"

He's surprised by my question. "What do you mean? About us?"

I nod.

"I don't even know your name," he confides with a slight smirk. "Are you famous?"

I slowly nod. "I used to be."

He shrugs, takes another deep look at me and says, "Nobody will know."

Although I've just met him, I sense that I can trust him.

14

Melody

I lead him toward my bedroom, still surprised by how nervous I feel. Can I really go through with this? Have him see my naked body – the jumbled clutter of scars? Sure, a lot of the damage from the fire has been repaired. But there are still so many imperfections.

"Is that a dog?"

I turn around. Mingus is whimpering from inside the bathroom we just passed.

"Yes."

"Do you want to let him out?" he asks.

"He's a puppy," I respond. "I just got him. I'm worried he might ruin the mood, you know?"

He looks at me a little surprised. "You're locking your puppy in a bathroom when you live in a house of this size?"

I don't know what to say. He's right. Mingus deserves to be treated better. "You're right. I'm being ridiculous."

I open the bathroom door. Mingus scrambles out and starts circling Kade's feet. Kade's face breaks into a grin as he looks at the puppy. He bends down and picks Mingus up. Mingus happily licks his face. Kade smiles – a real big smile, and the first I've seen from him. It shatters the somber presence he had earlier. His smile looks so genuine, so sincere. My attraction to him grows tenfold.

I really want to fuck this guy.

"Hey, little fella," Kade says to Mingus as the puppy continues licking his face. The tough exterior I saw when I first opened the door has vanished. I'm now staring at a gorgeous, well-built man holding a puppy. Kade's warmth and friendliness is palpable. "What's his name?" he asks, turning to me, smiling.

"Mingus," I reply, still shocked by his change in demeanor.

"After the jazz musician?"

I'm surprised he guessed right. Charles Mingus was an old-school jazz musician from the fifties and sixties.

"Yeah," I say with a nod.

"Cool." Kade raises Mingus and looks into his puppy eyes. "You've got a cool name after a cool dude, buddy." Mingus returns the compliment by lathering Kade's face with his tongue. Kade chuckles and lowers Mingus to the floor. When he straightens up, our eyes meet. I feel an electric shock. That's what his gaze does to me. It's like sex lightning!

I take a deep breath to calm myself and continue walking toward the bedroom; Mingus follows close behind.

It's been so long since I've had a man in my company – since I've felt a masculine presence in my home. I miss it. And even if I have to pay for it, I'll treasure it tonight.

When I get to the door, I turn around. "Okay, he can't follow us into the bedroom."

Kade looks down at the puppy and shrugs. "Sorry dude, she's the boss."

Mingus whimpers as we close the bedroom door on him. Once inside my room, I walk over to the stereo and put on music – to drown Mingus's whimpers from the hallway.

"*In This Special Place*," says Kade, recognizing the song.

"One of my favorite albums," I reply.

"Good fucking music, that's for sure," he says with an appreciative nod.

As the music fills the room, we stare at each other silently.

"So, how should we do this?" I ask, feeling a nervous knot in my stomach start to grow.

He takes a few slow steps forward.

"Would you feel more comfortable with the lights turned off?" he asks.

I nod gratefully. He walks over to the light switch and flicks it off. The moonlight streaming in through my bedroom window is now the only source of illumination. My guard comes down as comfort seeps in.

"Let's start off slow," he says as he returns to where I'm standing. "Why don't you just lay back on the bed and let me do all the work."

I like the sound of that. I take a seat on the bed and look up at him. Kade slowly slips off his t-shirt. I practically drool over the muscles rippling in his stomach then admire his chiseled chest. I haven't felt the hard body of a man in so long. He unbuckles his belt.

The nervous knot in my stomach eases and my body begins tingling with anticipation of what's to come.

Kade kicks off his chucks and pulls down his jeans. The only thing standing between his cock and me are a pair of white boxer briefs. My excitement grows. As I admire the tattoos running up his arms, I notice the portrait of a young boy tattooed on Kade's chest. The boy is smiling, a wide happy grin. I'm about to compliment the artwork, but then Kade steps toward me.

I notice his cock shift under his briefs. He reaches and pulls down his boxers. My heart catches in my throat at the sight of his impressive manhood. Instantly, my sex pulsates with need. Any hesitation I had disappears at the sight of his gorgeous cock.

I haven't been properly fucked in what feels like forever. I want it badly. I eagerly take his shaft in my hand, tugging on it. It grows harder with my caress. I raise my eyes and look up at Kade.

"You're blessed," I tell him.

"Thanks," he says with a slow, satisfied smile.

Slowly, I begin stroking his cock. It grows even larger. My eyes widen. I haven't had a cock this big in a really long time. And his is the perfect girth and size. I feel my pussy getting wetter just thinking about him sliding inside me.

I lean forward, desperately wanting to take his gorgeous shaft in my mouth. But I stop myself. I can't. Not with this mask on. It's covering my entire face. I lower my head in disappointment.

"This fuckin' mask," I mutter.

Kade senses my frustration because he responds, "Don't worry. We can work around it."

He reaches down, offering me his hand. I take it and stand back up.

"I thought we agreed that I'd do all the work anyway," he says.

He slowly reaches for the buttons on my chambray shirt. My heart beat races.

He's going to see the flawed skin on my chest!

I quickly grab his wrist. He stops then looks at me. That soulful sadness has returned to his gaze.

"Don't worry," he whispers. "We all have scars." His voice echoes the haunted turmoil of recent trauma. I realize that the only difference between Kade and I might be that my scars are visible and his hide underneath the surface.

I sense he understands my inner conflict because he might be going through his own. I knew there was a reason why I chose him.

He's haunted just like I am.

I breathe a sigh of relief as I realize I'm in very safe hands.

I let go of his wrist, letting him proceed.

He moves in closer. We're so close; we could kiss…

He unbuttons my shirt and gently slides it off my shoulders. I raise my arms above my head allowing him to pull off my black tank top. With adept fingers he unfastens my bra. Slowly and ever so gently, he begins running his strong, firm hands over my fragile skin, over my breasts. My body springs to life at the sensation of his touch. I rest my hand against his chest as he kisses the side of my neck. His warm lips against my tough, ropey skin are welcomed and needed.

He continues with a trail of kisses down my chest, taking one of my breasts in his mouth, gently tugging on my nipple. Lord, how I've missed a man's lips on my body, on my tits. I grab the back of his head and press it against my chest. His touch makes me forget all my inhibitions.

Kade drops to his knees. He looks at me as he runs his hands up my legs and under my peasant skirt.

My breath catches as I feel his fingers reach over the top of my undies. He slides them over my hips, and down my legs.

I help him by taking off my skirt. It drops to the floor. Except for my mask, I'm completely naked, just like him.

Kade gets back to his feet. He runs his fingers over my scarred skin, his digits delicately dancing across my flesh. He squeezes my shoulders, motioning me to turn around. He continues running his hands down my back. Then he squeezes my ass.

I feel his warm breath against the back of my neck as he whispers in my ear, "You have nothing to be ashamed of."

I struggle to stifle the emotion that suddenly overwhelms me. He may be lying, but I don't care. I appreciate his words and need to hear them. This isn't about sex anymore. His presence – here, in my bedroom – makes me feel alive again.

Kade moves closer, and I feel his cock, now fully erect, press against my backside.

"Here's the proof that you having nothing to be ashamed of," he says with a growl. "Do you feel how hard I am for you?"

I'm overcome with gratitude and desire. A tear rolls down my cheek. To be wanted this way, by another human being, is something I never thought I'd experience again.

Kade leans forward and wraps his strong arm around my waist. His fingers slide across my belly, toward my crotch. He begins to tease my wet lips with his fingers.

"You need this: me, inside you," he says in a low whisper.

"You have no idea," I reply, resting the back of my head against his shoulder, thankful for his presence.

"Well, the waits over," he growls and places another kiss on my shoulder.

Slowly, he turns me so I face him. I'm surprised by the lust and passion burning in his eyes. Could it really be for someone like me? I glance down at his rock-hard cock.

"Lie on the bed," he orders. "It's time I give you what you need."

Grateful, I follow his instructions.

Kade grabs a condom from his jeans and slips it on his cock. Then he climbs over me. I feel the tip of his cock nudge against my pussy.

I look into his dark, intense eyes and press my hands against his chest.

"You ready?" he asks.

I want to kiss his luscious lips, but can't. I simply nod.

Kade shifts his hips and I feel the head of his cock slowly part the lips of my pussy. He eases himself inside me. My pussy welcomes him, clenching around his girth.

"You feel good," Kade whispers into my ear.

"Trust me, you feel better," I confess.

Slowly, he pumps his cock in and then out. With each stroke my pussy throbs for more. I wrap my arms around his wide back, my legs around his waist. I want him deeper inside me. He's bigger than I'm used to, but I want to take as much of him as I can.

"Fuck yes," I moan with pleasure. "You don't know how badly I need this."

Kade increases his long, deep thrusts, each one raising my threshold of desire.

My breath quickens as we find our rhythm. Drops of pleasure slide down my thighs. Then I feel it coming. That sensation I've been missing for so long is slowly building inside me. I dig my nails into Kade's back as I wrap my legs tightly around his waist. I want all of him. As his cock stretches me wide, and fills me to the brim, I beat my fist against his back. "Fuck yeah, Kade. You feel fuckin' a-maz-ing."

Then it finally comes - the rush of joy, the heat of passion, coursing through my entire body.

I wail with utter abandon as the rising crescendo of *In This Special Place* fills the room. My pussy pulsates like a jackhammer. Gasping, I come all over Kade's cock.

But we're not finished yet. I'm still hungry.

15

KADE

When she opened the door, I was surprised to see she was wearing a white mask. She told me about her accident and the scars on her body. I had a hunch this meeting was going to be different than my other sessions.

Most of my clients are rich LA women who are cheating on their husbands.

She was different.

She was an accident survivor, longing to reconnect sexually.

Of everyone she could have picked online, she chose me. And when I saw her hiding behind a mask, I understood why. She wanted her first time since the accident to be with someone who could empathize with her loss and disappointment. That way, sex with a total stranger would feel a little less awkward. As I slowly pieced together her motivations, my mood changed. Earlier, my thoughts were preoccupied with sadness and regret. But when I realized this woman had experienced her own tragedy, I stopped thinking about my suffering and decided to do my best to alleviate hers.

If this woman wanted pleasure, I was committed to giving it to her.

When we stepped into her bedroom, I could tell she was nervous. I tried to make her more comfortable. At first, I thought our sex-capade would be slow and filled with hesitation. But the second this woman caught sight of my cock, the mood instantly changed. Her eyes lit up.

She wanted to get properly fucked.

After her first orgasm, she says, "That was a good start, but don't hold back. You don't have to be delicate. Make me feel like a real woman."

I raise her legs above her head and hold them together. She nods and I ease every inch of my cock into her.

"Fuck yes," she moans as she tilts her head back. She checks to make sure her mask hasn't shifted. When she's confident it's secure, she confesses, "Damn, you're huge."

"Do you want me to pull back?" I ask.

She shakes her head vigorously and checks her mask again. "No, I want more."

I pin her legs back, so I can go really deep.

Her moans grow louder.

I decide to go balls deep and her eyes widen behind her mask.

"That's it," she cries.

I increase my thrusts, my balls slapping against her ass.

She begs me not to stop.

As I continue driving myself into her, I release her legs. She quickly wraps them around me, pulling me into her. I wrap my arms around her and feel her warm body against mine. I feel the passion radiating from her skin.

"I need more," she gasps. "More of you..."

She orders me to fuck her from behind. With a growl of desire, I eagerly nod. I twirl her on to her stomach and pull her to her knees. She brings her hands to her mask once again, to make sure it hasn't moved.

I grab her ass cheeks and spread them wide. I ease my cock inside her.

"Give it to me, Kade," she shouts.

Gripping her ass, I unleash all of my manhood. I thrust my shaft, hard and deep into her wet cunt.

"More," she cries.

Damn, she really wants it. I feel like I'm in the ring, but instead of fighting, we're fucking. And this woman is taking me the distance.

The sadness that existed when we first met has vanished. Right now, in her bedroom, there's just the bliss of hot sex.

This chick is so in the moment – so in love with the sensation I'm giving her –that it's really turning me on, getting me harder. I run my hands over her scar-covered body. I can't imagine the suffering she's been through. But right now, I'm not noticing any of her scars. Like her, I'm caught up in the moment. It's electric. It's shocked me out of my stupor. As I plow my cock into her, I feel myself letting go. All my anger and frustration has been transformed into pure sexual energy. I'm giving her every last fuckin' drop.

"That's it," she cries. "Fuck me like you mean it."

She presses her ass toward me and I give it a firm smack, then I pull back on her hair.

"Yes!" she shouts.

She wants me to be even more forceful, really unleash, not hold back.

I grip her flesh, bite into her skin. I'm not thinking anymore. I just want to fuck her. I wrap my arm around her waist, then reach to squeeze her tits and pinch her pert nipple. The whole time, I plow her with deep, successive thrusts. Her pussy is so warm and wet, dripping with desire. I'm so fuckin' turned on. It's the first time in years that my mind isn't caught in some random feedback loop of misery. Right here, right now, with her body grinding against mine, I've forgotten everything else in my life. It's just me and her. This moment. It feels amazing.

I realize, we're not just fucking: we're both coming to life.

She locks her fingers with mine, and I feel her body tense. She's going to come again. I increase my thrusts, urging her toward the edge of bliss. I want to make sure she enjoys every second of this ride.

"Oh God! Oh God! Oh God!" She cries with joy.

I release her hand and lean back. I grab onto her ass cheeks and give her one good, hard thrust. Her pussy's grip on my cock tightens.

She shrieks with joy as she comes.

Then her head collapses on the bed. I ease my cock out of her. It's lathered with her sex juices. She turns around, quickly checks her mask, and looks at me. "Can I go for a ride?" she asks breathlessly.

This woman is awesome. She's still not satiated. I love it! I shoot her a smirk and say, "Sure thing. Let's go to the rodeo."

She gets up and pushes me back onto the bed.

With relish, she mounts me and begins rocking her hips back and forth.

"Thank you, Kade," she says, her voice filled with pleasure. "I fuckin' need this. You feel amazing inside me."

I reach up and squeeze her tits. As I feel her slick walls envelope my hard shaft, I realize how much I've needed this too. I feel like I'm connecting with another human being for the first time since Max's death. It's primal. It's pure.

As she rocks herself back and forth on my stiff rod, she shrieks with joy, and comes again.

After three orgasms, she finally needs a break. Like a fighter, she taps out. I stop to catch my breath as she collapses alongside me on the bed.

She turns to look at me. Through her mask, I see her eyes. They're bright, filled with a new life and joy that wasn't there before. I can't help but smile.

We both struggle to steady our breathing.

"Damn, that was awesome," I confess to her.

"You're a rock star," she says.

16

KADE

I must have fallen asleep. That never happens when I'm with a client. Usually, after we fuck, I get dressed, collect my money, and leave. But she asked me to stay a while. I saw how grateful she was for the orgasms I helped her achieve, so I agreed. And if I'm being honest, I wanted to chill for a moment too. I've never had sex like this before.

The longer we kept screwing, the more comfortable she got in her own skin. She lost herself in the moment, and stopped worrying about her scars. She didn't take off her mask, but other than that, she was unbridled.

It really turned me on.

But it wasn't just that. I felt comfortable around her, strangely at ease. I didn't feel the tension and anger I usually carry in my body.

Maybe that's why I fell asleep.

After fucking, we laid next to each other in bed. I felt so relaxed for the first time in ages that I must have drifted off. Still, that's no excuse. I'm never supposed to fall asleep with a client, especially in their home.

Sunlight streams through the bedroom window.

Shit, what time is it?

I get up and check my phone: 9 a.m.. I didn't just take a nap – I passed out! That's totally unprofessional. I quickly get dressed. As I throw on my t-shirt, I hear music, but the tune is not from the stereo in the bedroom. The bedroom door is open and the music is coming from somewhere else in the house. I throw on my sneakers and walk out of the room.

When I step into the living room, I see her. She's dressed in a black silk robe, sitting at a piano, her fingers dancing across the keys. It was her singing that I heard from the bedroom. The song is sad yet sweet. It's not a song I recognize, but the melody is one I immediately like. She hasn't noticed me standing in the corner. She's lost in the song, her voice flowing with such raw intensity and meaning, that it throws me off guard. Her voice is captivating. And the emotional lyrics hit me in the chest like a bullet of truth.

You try to lock it away, bury it down
Tell yourself it's lost and will never be found
But it's always there,
Under the surface, and under your skin

Suddenly, she stops singing and hastily picks up a pen resting on the piano. She jots something down on a piece of paper in front of her.

I can't believe it. I'm listening to an original. She's composing it right here on the spot. Who is this chick?

Mingus, the puppy, is resting on the floor near her feet. He notices me and yelps. The woman quickly turns on her piano bench and looks my way. Her hands dart to her mask to make sure it's on. She sighs with relief.

"Good Morning," I say. "I'm sorry I fell asleep. I shouldn't have done that. I'll get out of your way."

"No worries," she replies. Her voice sounds light, more vibrant than it did when we first met. She motions to the piano. "After our…" she pauses to find the right word. "I guess we can call it a session. After you fell asleep. I came out here and started working."

"You've been here all night?" I ask.

She slowly nods. "I got inspired."

"Cool," I say. We stare at each other. I wonder what she looks like under that mask. Her eyes, the only part I can see of her face, are animated, inviting. "Well, I guess I'll let you get back to work," I say when I feel like I've been staring at her far too long.

"Thanks," she says softly.

After a long pause, she turns back to the piano and begins playing with the keys. Then she notices I haven't left the room.

"Is there something…" She finally realizes. "Duh, I'm sorry. I have to pay you."

She hurries to a desk on the opposite end of the living room. She opens a drawer and approaches me with a stack of bills.

"Two thousand, right?"

I nod.

She counts out several hundred-dollar bills and hands them to me.

"That's too much," I say, noticing she has over-counted by at least a thousand.

"No, it isn't," she replies. "Consider it a bonus for going above and beyond what I hired you for. You just fucked me out of my stupor, Kade."

Our eyes meet again.

"Glad I could help," I say with a shrug. "But you don't have to do that. It's just two thousand."

"I insist," she replies. "Please."

She motions to me to take the money.

"Fine," I mutter. I'll be honest, for a brief moment last night, I forgot I was a whore. Now, it's back to reality. I take the wad of bills and stuff them in my back pocket. "You a song writer?" I ask.

"Yeah."

"Whatever you're working on, it sounds good."

"Thank you."

We keep staring at each other. I realize I've probably overstayed my welcome.

I glance at the puppy. "Take it easy, Mingus." He yelps a reply. Then I turn to her. "It was a pleasure meeting you."

"You too," she says softly, nodding her head.

Considering the night we just spent together, we awkwardly shake hands.

I leave the room and head toward the backdoor. When I swing the door open, I startle a redheaded woman with freckles standing outside. She's carrying a bag of groceries and has a set of keys in her hand.

"Who are you?" she asks suspiciously.

"I'm a friend of…" then I realize I don't even know her name. I see the suspicion grow in the redhead's eyes.

"She doesn't have any friends, except me," she blurts.

She rushes past me with her bag of groceries. She runs into the kitchen shouting, "Melody, are you alright?"

"I'm fine, Suzie! I'm in the living room working!"

So that's her name: Melody. It suits her.

The girl, named Suzie, turns to me. Her nervous suspicion is now replaced by a calmer, more curious look.

"A friend, huh?"

I shrug. "Yep."

Then I turn and walk out the door.

As I make my way through the gates, I notice the same red Volkswagen parked down the street. Except this time, I can clearly see that the dude sitting inside has a camera and is snapping pictures.

I think about approaching him but decide I should just go home. It's not my place to create a fuss.

When I hit the 110, I get stuck in traffic. Trapped in my car, I raise the volume on the radio and listen to one of the pop songs playing. It's a terrible song so I turn off the radio and think about her. About Melody. About the song she was composing.

Her voice sounded amazing.

Then I think about the night we just spent together. It wasn't like my normal fuck sessions. Usually, I just go through the motions with a client. With Melody, it was different. True, she just wanted sex from me. But it felt like it was connected to something much deeper.

I think I actually helped her last night. Like she needed something that only I was able to provide. There was a connection between us. I wonder if she sensed the hollow feeling I've been carrying around since Max died.

I wonder if she felt that I was lonely, just like her.

I couldn't see her face, but I could see her eyes. They contained a multitude of emotions. Besides sadness and loneliness, they also reflected a fire, a burning desire. A hunger. A need.

The way she fucked, I can tell she's a passionate person. I guess you would have to be, if you're an artist. And when I think about that beautiful song she was writing, I can tell she's talented.

Last night, for the first time in ages, I wasn't thinking about Max. I was focused on what I could do to make Melody more comfortable in her skin. I think I helped her move one step forward. She needed to connect to someone, that person happened to be me.

I'm surprised by how badly I needed it too.

After Max died, I've been struggling to find a reason to continue living. I felt like my presence on this earth didn't really matter.

Last night, with Melody, it mattered.

I mattered.

17

*K*ADE

Early the next morning, I get a call from someone who found me on Shane's website. She wants to book me for a session – immediately – but wants to meet at the strangest of places.

"I'm sorry, did you say Denny's?" I ask, not sure I heard her correctly.

"Yes. On Santa Monica and Highland. Can you be there by 8 am?"

"Um, sure, but I'm not going to have sex with you there, right?" The last thing I need is to get busted for having sex in a public place.

"Of course not," she replies, sounding flustered. "Just meet me there. I'll be at one of the booths in the back."

"Okay. What do you look like?"

"Don't worry about it. I'll spot you when you walk in."

She hangs up on me.

I sigh. I'm not in the mood for a session, especially this early. Maybe this woman wants to spend two thousand dollars eating breakfast with me? As long as I get paid, that's fine by me.

Plus, I'm hungry.

An hour later, I step into Denny's. I'm surprised to see the woman I bumped into yesterday – the one carrying groceries – wave at me from a table. Her name's Suzie, if I remember correctly.

"You?" I say with a smirk as I approach her.

She looks around the restaurant, nervous. She's wearing large sunglasses and a Dodgers baseball cap. If she's trying to look inconspicuous, she's not doing a very good job.

"Sit down," she whispers.

I take a seat across from her.

"Does your friend know you called me?" I ask.

"Of course she does," Suzie replies, like it's the dumbest question on earth. "She's the reason I'm here."

I look at her confused. I lean in and whisper, "You guys want to do a threesome?"

Embarrassed, Suzie lowers her head. She tries to hide her face by pulling down her baseball cap as a waitress approaches. I order French toast. The waitress pours me some coffee. When the waitress leaves, Suzie leans forward.

"No," she whispers, her voice flat. "We do not want to have a threesome. Melody wants me to propose something to you."

"Okay," I say, slightly relieved. Don't get me wrong, threesomes are fun, but it's really early in the morning. "What's the proposal?" I ask.

Suzie looks around cautiously. She leans in closer to make sure nobody overhears us. "She wants to enlist your services again."

I'm confused. "Then why doesn't she use the website,

like last time?"

Suzie leans back in her chair and takes a sip from her coffee. "Well, that's the thing. What happened the other night was a mistake. She shouldn't have used a website like that. She had a few too many to drink and wasn't thinking clearly. You see, Melody has a reputation to protect. She needs to be more discreet moving forward. If we could just deal with you directly, without going through a website, that would be preferable."

"Alright," I reply. I don't see how that will be much of a problem. As long as I get paid, and Shane gets his money, that's all that matters.

"There's something else I would like to discuss," says Suzie. "Melody wants you exclusively."

"What do you mean?"

"That you engage in your um… activities with her, and only her. You lose all your other clients."

I shake my head. "Nah. That can't happen."

Suzie moves forward and whispers, "She's willing to pay handsomely for the privilege of being your only client."

"Really?" I say somewhat surprised.

Suzie nods and continues to speak in a hushed tone. "It appears you've made quite an impression on her. You see, Mr.?"

"Kade."

"Well, Mr. Kade – "

"Not Mr. Kade. Just Kade."

"What?" She looks at me confused.

"My name is Kade."

"Well, Kade, whatever you did to her the other night

really made an impact. That song she was writing, while you were leaving…"

"Yeah. It was good," I say.

"Very good." Suzie agrees with a nod and smile. She leans back in her chair and takes another sip of coffee. She eyes me and says, "Melody hasn't written a song in over a year. And she's convinced that you had something to do with her breakthrough."

"Me?" I say, surprised.

"I tried convincing her that it's the puppy," says Suzie with a shrug. "But she insists it's you. She wants to keep seeing you. She thinks you might inspire her to write more songs."

"And she wants to keep fucking, right?"

Suzie lowers her head and shakes it. "Please, keep your voice down."

I apologize, even though I don't think anyone is listening to us.

Suzie clears her throat. "Yes. She wants to continue to engage in those… um… activities… with you."

I take a sip of coffee and lean back in the booth. I'm surprised by the offer. I didn't see any of this coming. "Well, to engage in those activities on an exclusive basis won't come cheap," I tell her. "How long does she want to see me?"

Suzie shrugs. "Depends on how long it takes her to write an album."

"Seriously?"

Suzie nods.

"Well, how long does that take, usually?"

Suzie shrugs again and takes another sip of coffee.

"You can't really put a time table on creativity," she replies. "We were thinking we would put you on a monthly retainer. Whenever Melody needs you, she calls you. Would one hundred thousand dollars a month be sufficient?"

I nearly spit out my coffee. If Melody takes six months to write her album, I'll be able to pay off my entire debt to Shane. I force myself to act cool. The one thing I've learned from dealing with Shane is: never take the first offer.

"I was thinking something closer to one-fifty," I say, trying to keep my enthusiasm hidden while desperately hoping I'm not blowing the deal.

Suzie shrugs. "How about we just agree to two hundred thousand a month, and everyone's happy."

My jaw nearly drops. "That works," I say with a slow nod. I'm trying to act like it's no big deal. But inside me, my heart is pounding like a sledgehammer.

"Great," says Suzie. She reaches into her purse and takes out a stack of papers. She plops them on the table between us.

"What's this?"

"A non-disclosure," she says, pushing the papers toward me. "By signing it, you agree to never tell anyone about your relationship with her. Otherwise, we can take you to court and sue you until you're dead broke. And there's something else in addition to the non-disclosure."

"What?" I ask as I flip through the pages.

"Melody wants you to get tested."

"STDs?"

Suzie nods. "If you're clean, she would like to move

forward in your activities without protection."

I shrug. "For two hundred thousand a month, that won't be a problem."

"Good," says Suzie. "Now give me your phone number. That way we can contact you directly. You can drop off the contract the next time you and her meet."

After I give her my cellphone number, she gets up from the table. She swings her purse over her shoulder.

"You're not eating breakfast?" I ask.

She shakes her head. "I had a green juice." She lowers her glasses and shoots me a curious look. "You're hot, I'll give you that. But for two hundred thousand, you better be amazing in the sack." She pushes her sunglasses up the ridge of her nose. "Melody will be in touch." Then, she walks out of the restaurant.

As I flip through the pages of the contract, the waitress appears with my French toast.

"Eating alone?" she asks.

"Looks that way," I reply. "But listen, would you mind putting in an order for the Heavy Man special."

The waitress gives me a smirk. "Hungry, huh?"

"I've been starving for years," I say with a grin. "Now, I can finally feed myself."

"Coming right up, sweetie," She walks toward the kitchen and places my order.

18

KADE

I drop down on the mat and look up at the kid. Luke, one of my trainers, has him in a triangle choke, one of the best submissions move in MMA fighting. The kid, whose name is Rico, recently joined my gym and doesn't know what to do now that he's trapped. His head is locked between three limbs – his arm and Luke's two legs.

"Now in this position," I tell the kid. "Once Luke has your legs locked, he can start applying pressure. If you don't tap out, you'll lose consciousness."

Rico taps out. Luke releases him from the hold.

"So, I'm basically fucked," says Rico, as he stands up and catches his breath.

I shake my head. "Not necessarily. If you keep calm and you're quick enough, you can find a way out of it. Let me show you."

I motion Luke to step forward. I bend down, and he places me in a triangle choke. I begin my instruction.

"You have a lot more options before he locks his legs in place. But let's say you're caught off guard. Lock your legs, Luke." Luke locks his legs behind my neck. "Now, there still might be a way out of it. The important thing is to relax your muscles and breathe. When you're not clear headed, you're fucked. See how Luke has me bent forward?"

"Yeah," says Rico.

"Well, what I'm going to do is take my trapped arm, move it forward, and place it on the opposite side of his head. Then, I'm going to come up on my feet and drive forward." I nod to Luke, signaling my move. I raise myself onto my feet. "Then, I'm going to take my knee and drive it into the side of his hip." I perform the move in slow motion so Rico can follow. "Then, I step over his head with my leg and spin my whole body to the far side of his head. I wrap my arm around his neck and turn him flat on his back. Now, I'm in control."

"That's awesome," says Rico, surprised by my ability to maneuver out of the position and gain the advantage.

I release Luke from the side mount, and we both stand up. "Thanks, Luke."

"No problem, boss."

Someone claps behind me. I turn and see Shane staring at us. His two bodyguards, Vince and Leo, are with him. I nod.

Shane points at Rico and grins. "You better be paying attention, kid. Kade could have been one of the greatest if life hadn't gotten in the way."

I turn to Rico and say, "Alright, that's enough for today. See you Wednesday."

I step off the mat and approach Shane.

"What's up?"

"Same old shit," he says.

I nod to Vince and Leo. "What's up, fellas?" They both just stare at me.

Shane motions me to follow him. We head to my office. Vince and Leo stay outside as I close the door.

"Those two don't talk much," I remark.

"I don't pay them to talk," says Shane. "I don't even think Leo speaks English. Not even Spanish. He's Russian. I'm not sure he even speaks that from what I can tell. I think he's an idiot, or a mute, or both. Nevertheless, he's a badass motherfucker. I saw him gouge a guy's eyes with his bare fingers then choke him to death. That's the kind of guy you want on your side."

"What about Vince?" I ask.

Shane shrugs. "He's shy. Lets his gun do most of the talking."

"Good to know," I reply as I approach my desk. I slide open a drawer and remove an envelope. I hand it to Shane.

Shane sits a hip on my desk and begins counting his money.

He shoots me a look. "You're short a G," he says.

"Yeah, I know. When I got there, she said all she could pay me was a thousand. I figure some money was better than no money."

I don't want to tell Shane about my meeting with Suzie and the agreement we came to regarding Melody, not until everything has been set in stone and I know the money is legit. I'm lucky Melody overpaid me by a thousand dollars on my first visit, because I would have had a hard time explaining to Shane how I met with Suzie but came back with nothing. There's only one thing Shane cares about these days: and that's money.

He closes the envelope and slaps it against his hip. He stands up from my desk. He's clearly annoyed he hasn't gotten the full amount.

"Alright, but don't let it happen again. We're not running a fuckin' charity here. If these bitches want your cock, they're going to have to pay for it."

I nod.

Shane places the envelope in his jacket pocket. I notice he's wearing another fine tailored suit that probably cost him more than two grand. The sparkling watch around his wrist probably cost five times that. If you saw him on the street, you'd probably think Shane was an investment banker and not one of LA's biggest gangsters.

I think Shane helped with Max's medical bills to even the score between us. It's crazy to think we were childhood friends, or that I took a bullet meant for him when we were kids. Now that we're older, Shane's grown colder. I guess you don't rise to his position in the underground world by being sentimental.

I suspect Shane has ordered some hits in his life. It wouldn't surprise me if he even did some of the killing himself. He was never the type to shy away from the dirty business of street life. He never talks about that with me, though. The less I know, the better.

"How you feeling?" he asks.

I shrug. "Alright."

"How's the leg? Back to normal?"

I nod. I don't have the range of motion I had before it snapped in the fight. But I'm mobile enough.

"You feel like kicking some ass?" Shane asks. I see a

glint in his eye.

I cock an eyebrow. "What are you talking about?"

Shane walks past me and takes a seat in the chair behind me. He plops his shiny black shoes on my desk. I guess technically, it's his desk, since he owns the gym now. That was part of the deal I made with him when he paid for Max's treatment. Now, I only get paid a small stipend to train people.

"I'm talking about you fighting this Saturday," he says. "Marco pulled out."

Marco is one of the guys I train. He's a good fighter. This weekend he was supposed to face Mitch Cork, an Irish dude, in one of Shane's underground matches. It's taking place at a warehouse in Venice.

"What happened?"

Shane shrugs. "His mom passed away. Says he can't fight. You want in?"

I shake my head. "That only gives me five days to train. Remember what happened last time?"

Shane points his finger at me. "What happened last time was that your mind wasn't on the fight but on your boy, Max."

Whenever someone speaks his name, I feel a rush of anguish charge through me. I take a breath and fight back the overwhelming feeling. "Yeah," I say with a nod.

"You don't have that on your mind anymore," says Shane as tactfully as he can. "Kade, when I told that runt out there that you could have been one of the greatest, I wasn't lying. It's too bad you had to take care of your boy because that bitch skipped town on you. That's why you started this gym, right? So you could be around for Max.

You put being a father above your career, which I honestly think was a dumb move."

I'm unable to speak. I'm fighting back the remorse running through me.

Shane stands up, oblivious to what I'm going through. "Well, now that he's gone, let's get you back to fighting. You still got some fighting years in that body of yours."

"I don't think it's a good idea," I mutter.

"Let me decide if it's a good idea, alright," Shane says. He stares at me. He's thinking something then sighs. "How about this?" he eventually says. "You fight this weekend, and a couple of the other fights I got lined up, and I'll knock a hundred grand off what you owe me."

I'm stunned by his proposal.

If my deal with Melody checks out, and Shane keeps his word, I'll be debt free much sooner than I expected. I won't be Shane's whore anymore. I'll finally be a free man.

"You're serious? A hundred grand off my debt?"

Shane slowly nods. "Fight this weekend and a couple of others I got lined up."

The thought of being debt free is an opportunity I can't pass up.

"Can I get the word out that you're fighting this Saturday?" Shane asks.

I nod. "Let's do it."

He slaps my back and heads toward the door.

"Just one thing," I tell him as he's about to leave.

He turns around.

"I can't do any sessions for the website this week. I've only got five days to train."

Shane hesitates for a moment. I can tell he doesn't like my request but agrees.

"Fine, but you better win, Kade. Cause now you're costing me money."

He opens the door and motions to Vince and Leo that it's time to go.

19

Melody

As I listen to the playback on the last song I recorded, I realize I'm breaking new ground. The lyrics are more thoughtful, the music more ambitious. The label probably won't like the direction I'm heading in. I assume they want something more pop-like.

Randy says I'm contracted to deliver an album of at least twelve songs. The contract doesn't mention that the label has to like them. So, if that's the case, I don't have to write songs that I think will be popular. I can spend my time writing songs that I actually think are good.

These last couple of days, the songs have just been pouring out of me. I'm spending most of my days and nights in my home studio, recording myself playing the piano, strumming guitar, and layering in beats. I've just finished song number five and I *really* like it. I'll listen to it again tomorrow. I just have to remind myself not to tinker on the song as much as I used to.

I've always been a perfectionist.

And when it comes to my music, I inevitably hear mistakes. Good is never good enough. A song can always be made to sound better. After the accident, my therapist, Jeannie, said that was something I needed to work on. I needed to stop chasing perfection and just let things be. At first, I thought she was talking about my appearance. But now I realize it might also apply to my music. After all, sometimes it's the minor imperfections in a song that make it memorable. Maybe Jeannie wasn't a terrible therapist after all. Too bad I fired her.

I step out of my recording studio and make my way to the piano in my living room. At the piano is where I usually discover a song. Taking a seat, I begin playing with the keys and close my eyes. I let myself settle into the moment, into my own breath. I treat this like a form of mediation. I don't force anything to come; I just let whatever wants to bubble to the surface make its way to my fingertips or my lips.

What flashes through my inner landscape are images of Kade. My lips curl into a smile as I remember his face, his body. That fella was exactly what the doctor ordered. He's hot, dark and mysterious: a killer combination. And most importantly, he knew how to be with a woman. He knew how to stay in the moment, and be just the right amount of rough. The sex wasn't mechanical. It didn't feel like he was auditioning for a porn movie, which is the case with a lot of the young studs today. It was passionate, hot and dirty. While we were fucking, I got the impression Kade actually appreciated my body, like he wanted to savor it and not just fuck. With all these damn scars, I wasn't expecting that at all. I'm still surprised by how comfortable I felt in his presence, especially when I was naked, my scars in plain sight. There's more to this guy than just a tough exterior and a ripped body. He has presence, depth.

Suzie tried to convince me it was Mingus that brought forth my recent inspiration. I have to admit, I like having Mingus in my life. But I know deep down that cuddly puppy isn't the reason for my creative spurt. It's Kade. His presence awoke something in me. After having sex with him, I felt like a woman again and not the victim of a horrible accident. I know I can never go back to being the old Melody, but Kade's alpha energy woke me up. He brought forth a desire that made me realize I'm still living, breathing, flesh. I'm still horny and desire a man's touch. Kade fucked me with care and made me grateful to still be alive. After months of contemplating suicide, that's a big fuckin deal.

Now, if I could just get the courage to leave this house and face the world again... *Baby steps, Melody.*

I play with the piano keys a bit more then open my eyes. I glance at the television hanging on the wall and am surprised to see my face on TV. Not my new face, but the pre-accident version of me. I marvel at my unblemished skin, my perfect nose and chin, my luscious lips.

Damn, I used to be hot.

I reach for the remote resting on the piano and unmute the television.

"It's been more than a year since pop sensation, Melody Swanson, has been seen in public," comments the entertainment news anchor. "After suffering a horrifying car crash, sources say she's turned into a recluse and refuses to leave her Hollywood Hills mansion. But it appears the reclusive star is taking in some late-night visitors. Recent photos show a mysterious man visiting Melody's mansion late at night and not leaving until early the following morning. Who is he? Call into our station if you have any leads. Because like we always say here at StarCentral: 'You have a right to know'."

I click off the television and sigh. "No, you don't have a right to know," I groan. I start wondering whether signing Kade to a contract was a bad idea. The last thing I want to deal with are paparazzi swarming my house again. After the accident, they were camped outside my home every day for months. Only the last three months or so have been relatively civil.

I glance at the floor. "What do you think, Mingus? Should I stop seeing him?"

I'm surprised Mingus isn't in his usual spot, near my feet. Then I hear him barking in the distance. I get up and make my way to the kitchen. Mingus is scratching the backdoor and jumping up and down. He needs to go outside.

I shake my head, disappointed with myself. I've been so obsessed with my music the last couple of hours that I've completely forgotten to take him out. I'm grateful he hasn't made a mess on my floor. I run back to my bedroom and slip on my mask. Then I grab Mingus's leash. When he sees me, he starts yapping excitedly.

"You really have to go, huh buddy?"

Mingus barks a reply. I snap the leash around his collar and open the door. Mingus immediately yanks me out with him. I'm relieved high bushes surround my backyard, providing much needed privacy.

Mingus drags me all over the yard, looking for the perfect spot to do his business. As he sniffs one place after another, I think about Kade again. Should I stop what I was planning with him? What if the media finds out he's an escort? It would ruin my reputation. But then again, my reputation has already been ruined. That car accident killed off the old Melody. She's never coming back. Nobody is going to want to see my new face on television, much less pay to see me on tour. From this moment forward, what should matter is what I want, what I need. And right now, I need him. I need to see him again.

Suddenly, I hear a noise coming from one of the bushes. Someone is shuffling around behind them. I pull on Mingus's leash. "Mingus, come." But he's too busy sniffing the ground around him to obey me. The rustling behind the bushes grows louder.

"Damn it," I hear a man curse.

Someone's on my property! He's hiding in my bushes!

I freak out. I drop Mingus's leash and run inside. I head straight to my bedroom and grab the gun from my nightstand. Flashbacks to that crazy guy, James, that I found in my kitchen years ago race through my mind. I can't take any chances. Holding the gun, my hands tremble with fright. I run back through my kitchen. I've never fired it. But there's always a first time for everything.

When I rush outside, I see him. He's in the middle of my backyard and Mingus is snapping at his legs.

My heart catches in my chest. I can't believe it.

It's him: Charlie, that paparazzi motherfucker.

The guy who followed me during the night of the accident is standing in my backyard; the son-of-a-bitch who took pictures of me while I was burning up in flames; the asshole, who rather than help me out of my car and save my life, was more interested in taking pictures of my impending death.

With his camera slung over his shoulder, he's trying to calm Mingus down. Mingus must sense Charlie's an asshole because he won't leave him alone. He's growling and trying to bite him.

"Easy fella," Charlie hisses.

"Get the fuck away from my dog!" I shout as I point my gun at him.

Charlie looks up. He's about to snap a picture. But when he sees the gun, his eyes widen, and he quickly lowers his camera.

"Get the fuck off my property, or I swear to God I'll shoot your head off."

My hands are still shaking, but I mean every word. There's one person I wouldn't hesitate to kill; and it's this grizzly bearded motherfucker.

"Go!" I scream. With my gun still raised and pointed at him, I take several steps forward. Charlie quickly turns around and runs back into the bushes. His large frame vanishes. I listen closely as he scurries away.

When I'm sure he's gone, I breathe once again. My heart is pounding in my chest. Mingus comes to my side, dragging his leash behind him. I quickly scoop him up. With Mingus in one hand, and my gun in the other, I hurry inside. I close the door and make sure the alarm is on.

I'm a bundle of nerves. Why won't the paparazzi just leave me alone? Particularly that asshole? It's like his mission is to ruin my life. Now, I regret not shooting him when I had the chance.

Mingus yelps.

"Whatever, he deserves it," I tell him.

I place Mingus down, unfasten his leash, and walk to my bedroom. I put the gun back in the drawer and take a seat on my bed. My hands are still shaking. I think about calling the police and telling them that Charlie trespassed onto my property. But then I realize that would only bring on more media attention. That's the last thing I want.

I'm frightened. Feeling vulnerable. I really don't want to be alone right now. I pull my cellphone out of my jacket pocket. I'm about to call Suzie and tell her what happened, ask her to come over. But I stop myself. I realize who I really want to call is him. I want him here, by my side. I want to feel his strong arms around me. I want to feel safe, protected, not alone.

If they get pictures of him coming over, I'll only be providing more fodder to the very paparazzi I loathe. But I don't care. I'm sick and tired of being by myself. The other night, with him, was the first time I've been happy since the accident.

Fuck, the paparazzi. I'm tired of them ruling my life.

I dial his number.

As the phone rings, I take a deep breath. When he answers and says hello, I'm surprised by how nervous I suddenly feel. Then I realize how foolish I'm being. After all, I just offered him a contract to have sex with me.

"It's me, Melody," I finally say.

He sounds taken off guard and takes a moment to respond.

"Hey, how's it going?" he asks.

Just hearing his voice calms me a little. He sounds strong, tough.

"Am I calling at a bad time?"

"No. Not at all."

I'm waiting for him to say more, but he doesn't. There's a long silence.

"Have you had a chance to think over what Suzie presented to you?" I finally ask.

"Yeah."

"And?"

"It sounds good."

Kade isn't much of a talker. But I don't care. I just want his strong presence in my life right now. And I'll take his body while I'm at it.

"Good. And what about getting tested?" I ask.

"I already have. I've got the results. All clear."

A smile quickly forms on my lips.

"That means we can begin our arrangement immediately." I'm somewhat surprised by the excited tone in my voice.

He doesn't respond.

"Is there a problem?" I ask.

"No. No problem. It's just that I have to train for a fight this weekend. Any chance we can meet at night?"

"Like tonight?" I put forth.

"Damn, that's fast," he says.

I know it is. But I really don't want to spend the night alone. What if Charlie comes back onto my property? But that's not the only reason I want Kade to come over. I wasn't exaggerating when I said Kade awoke something in me. After having sex with him, I felt alive for the first time since the accident. I don't want that feeling to end. "I know it's last minute, Kade," I say into the phone. "But can you be at my place at 9 pm and bring the signed contract?"

There's a long pause. *Please say yes. I need to see you.*

"Sounds good," he finally says.

Nervous energy rushes through me. My body eagerly anticipates round two with the hot and gorgeous Kade.

"Oh, one more thing," I tell him before getting off the phone. "Could you wear a hoodie?"

"I usually do," he replies. "But why?"

Sighing, I tell him, "There's some paparazzi lurking around my house. You might want to keep your face hidden when you come over. I hope that's not a problem?"

"Not at all," he says. "Especially considering what you're paying me."

We hang up. I take off my mask and smile. I'm really looking forward to seeing him again. I remind myself that this is a business transaction. There's a contract for crying out loud. He's being paid to have sex with me. This is all a fantasy. But after everything I've been through, I allow myself to get temporarily lost in the illusion.

I take a seat at the piano. Although running into that asshole Charlie has really riled me, I need to get back to work. I close my eyes and try to calm my breathing. I try to go back to that quiet place, where I forget the world outside and just focus on what's going on below the surface of who I am.

The first image to pop into my head is of him. I just can't stop thinking about him. His eyes. His strong, capable hands.

Then, I remember the tattoo of a young boy inked on his chest. I wonder if he has a son. Then, it hits me out of nowhere – like a freight train – the thought of having children. I've always wanted to be a mother. But I thought it was something I could put off until I was in my thirties. After all, I had a career to establish first. But now, with the accident, I wonder if I'll ever get married and have children. Who would want to settle down with someone like me? Someone who looks the way I do? Has this accident robbed me of more than just my looks and my career?

I force myself to stay focused and not let these thoughts derail me. I've finally started to work again and it feels good. If I'm going to allow these scary thoughts to the surface, I need to transfer them into music and not let them drag me back to bed.

I start writing another song.

20

KADE

Paparazzi? Damn, what have I gotten myself into? But for two hundred thousand dollars and the chance to pay off my debt to Shane, whatever it is, it's worth it.

When I get off the phone with Melody, I finish my sparring session with Luke. Five days isn't enough training time, but Shane had a point. The last time I fought, I was such an emotional wreck that my mind wasn't focused. I was more worried about Max than my opponent in the cage. That's why I lost.

That won't be the case this time.

After finishing my training session, I leave the gym and go back to my apartment to shower and get ready for my meeting with Melody.

As I drive my Corolla up the 110, I glance at the signed contract on the passenger seat. It's still hard to believe our paths have crossed again. After meeting with Suzie at Denny's, and going through the contract, I finally realized who I spent the night with.

Melody Swanson.

She's a big pop star whose music was constantly on the radio a few years ago. I'm not a big fan of pop music but her stuff was pretty good. I prefer hip-hop and R&B. Melody was also in a movie I saw at Layla's place. It was some chick flick that Layla loved but wasn't really my thing. I'm an action-heist-film kind of guy. I did some research online and discovered that after her accident, Melody was rushed to the same hospital where Max was staying. She was the reason there were all those paparazzi roaming around the night I lost my fight. I vaguely remember Shane mentioning something when he came to the hospital for a visit. But my mind must have been such a jumbled up mess that it didn't register. Now, Melody's life and mine have intersected once again.

This deal with Melody will help me pay off my debt. And by agreeing to a couple of fights for Shane, I'm getting closer to being a free man. It's a shame I don't own my gym anymore, because then I would have a semblance of my life back. I built that gym with blood, sweat, and tears. But in exchange for the money to help pay Max's medical bills, I had to sign it over to Shane. Maybe one day I can get it back. At least I hope.

When I pull my car onto Melody's street, I see that same red Volkswagen parked outside her house. In the darkness, I notice the silhouette of a man pointing his camera lens at me. I pull my hoodie over my head to cover my face. Rather than park on the street, I drive up to the gate and roll down my window. I press the button on the intercom. I tell Melody it's me, and the gates open. I drive my car up her driveway.

She opens the door wearing her mask. She's sporting a long sleeve Rolling Stones t-shirt and leggings. I considered wearing something nicer than jeans and a t-shirt but that's not really me. I'm a jeans-and-t-shirt kind of guy.

"There's a guy parked on your street taking pictures," I tell her.

"I should have shot him when I had the chance," she hisses through her mask. She motions me inside.

We enter the kitchen.

"Shot who?" I ask, surprised by her statement.

"That paparazzi asshole," she says, annoyed. "I caught him in my backyard earlier today."

"You call the cops?"

She shakes her head. "It's not worth all the attention. I thought when I pointed my gun at him; he'd get the hint. But this guy is a real pest. He just won't leave me alone."

I realize as she tells me this, that Melody is a prisoner in her own home – confined to her house. This, compounded with her accident, must make her really lonely. I understand why she called me. She wants my company tonight, and it's not just about sex.

"Can I get you anything: water, beer?" she offers.

"I'm good. Where's Mingus?" I ask.

"He wore himself out attacking that paparazzi," she says. "He's sleeping in the living room."

She glances at the stack of papers in my hand. I hand her the contract. She flips through the pages, noting where I have signed and then looks at my test results.

"I'm sorry for all this," she says. "I just need to be careful."

"No worries," I say with a shrug.

She eyes me through her mask. "Well, now you know who I am."

I nod.

"I'm not that person anymore," she says. "But the media still seems interested in me. They just want to snatch pictures of my fucked up face so they can make a few bucks." She sighs then says, "I should warn you: if you and I continue to see each other, there's a chance the media might discover who you are? Do you have a problem with that?"

I shrug. "You're paying me two hundred thousand dollars a month," I respond. "It's worth the risk."

"I see," she says glancing at the contract. I sense a disappointed tone in her voice. But then she shifts gears and turns more business-like. "You realize by signing this contract, you can't tell anyone, anything about our relationship? If you even try to profit from it – "

I raise my hand and cut her off. "Don't worry about that. I ain't that type. I can't stand any of this Hollywood bullshit." I'm not lying. Sometimes, I wonder if I'd be happier living up in Portland. But I was born and raised in LA. Even though this city can get annoying at times, it's in my blood. But the Hollywood-celebrity aspect of it never interested me.

I try to put Melody at ease regarding the whole thing and say, "As far as I'm concerned, it sounds like we both need each other right now. You need me to keep fucking you so you stay inspired, and write your music…"

" – And you need my money," she says, finishing my thought. There's that disappointed tone again. But this time there's an edge to it.

"Speaking of money," she continues, in that business-like manner. "How about I pay you one hundred thousand up front and the remainder at the end of the month? We can continue that kind of payment schedule until I'm no longer in need of your services."

I shrug. "Works for me."

She nods. "Good. I'll have Suzie wire you the money tomorrow."

Damn, just like that I'll have all that money in my bank account. Too bad I have to turn around and give it straight to Shane.

Melody keeps staring at me with her vivid green eyes. It's hard to guess what she's thinking because I can't read her facial expressions. She's still hiding behind the mask. But I definitely notice a change in her tone, particularly when it comes to talking about the contract. Maybe she's annoyed because she feels the need to pay someone to sleep with her. Maybe she wishes money wasn't involved in this arrangement.

"Your friend says you've been writing songs," I say, trying to fill the silence.

"I have," she says with a sigh. "That's why you're here. I'm under contract to deliver a final album to my label. Then I'm a free woman."

"Sounds like you and I have a lot in common," I reply.

"How's that?" she asks, tilting her head.

"Well, because of our arrangement," I explain, "I might be able to get out of something."

I don't want to go into all the details.

"Then it's a good thing we found each other," she says.

I nod. "Yeah, I guess you could say that."

There's a long, awkward silence.

"Well then, should we..." she begins to say.

I assume she's busy and wants to get things started. I unzip my hoodie and begin taking off my t-shirt.

"Hold on a second, Kade," she says. "I don't want you to fuck me in my kitchen. Not yet anyway."

I shrug. "Sorry. I thought you might be busy and want to get started. My bad." I pull my t-shirt back down. "What did you have in mind?" I ask.

"I've got some ideas," she says.

Although I can't see her face, the tone in her voice tells me she's thinking something wicked.

21

KADE

Her pussy tastes delicious. I run my tongue over her wet, succulent lips, suck on her clit, and savor her juice. She tastes as sweet as a peach, so fuckin' good.

She grabs the back of my head and grinds it against her pussy. The smell of her sex filters through my nose. She smells like spring – but bless her – she fucks like a hot, dirty summer.

"Damn, Kade, you're fuckin' good with your tongue," she moans.

She's sitting on top of her piano. I have her legs parted wide. We're both naked, and I can't wait to slide my rock hard cock into her wet cunt.

She must want the same thing because she yanks my head back and stares down at me.

"I need your cock," she moans, her voice brimming with desire.

I raise myself, so I can stare into her eyes. She's still wearing the mask. She won't take it off.

I feel a tug and glance down. Her hand is wrapped around my cock. I'm so aroused; I think I might come.

"Easy," I tell her. "You've got me so hard, I'm about

to blow."

She swiftly removes her hand. "Oh no," she says. "We can't have that. This is just round one."

I wrap my arm around her and lift her off the piano. I guide her legs around my waist. She wraps her arms around my neck. I hold her up by her hips, over my cock. Through the mask, I stare into her eyes.

"What is it?" she asks.

"You really turn me on," I growl.

Slowly, I lower her onto my cock. I feel her lips part and welcome me inside.

Melody closes her eyes and rests her head against my shoulder. "Damn, that's fuckin' good," she moans. I glide her up and down my cock, each time pushing myself a little further.

Her moans grow louder. "Give it all to me, Kade," she cries.

Holding her as I stay standing, I slide into her tightness. When I'm finally balls deep, I give a hard shove of my hips.

"Deeper," she shouts.

I smirk. Melody and I share the same belief: If you're going to do something, go the distance. I lift her off my cock and drop her legs to the ground. She looks at me, her eyes sparkling with life. I can't wait to give her what she needs. I quickly whirl her around, so her back is facing me. I push her forward, so her upper body is draped over the grand piano.

I run my hands over her scarred back; then ease the head of my cock inside her. She widens her stance so she can take all of me in. I grip one of her hips as I continue running my other hand over her back.

"You feel fuckin' amazing," she exclaims with joy.

I thrust my pelvis forward, my cock tingling with pleasure as it stretches her wide.

"So do you," I tell her. And it's the truth. Her pussy fits my cock like the perfect glove. I continue my thrusts and run my hand up and down her back. As I pound her with my cock, and she begs me to continue, there's no other place I'd rather be.

22

Melody

We finish round four in the bedroom, collapse on the bed, both of us catching our breath.

"I don't think I'm going to be able to walk for weeks," I exclaim.

"Was I too rough?" he asks.

I turn and look at him. "It can never be too rough with me, Kade."

I lose myself in his gaze, and I notice a smirk cross his lips. I want to kiss him, but I can't. I don't want to deal with the awkwardness of removing my mask, or the possibility he might cringe at the sight of my face. It would destroy the illusion of what we have. I don't want to ruin a good thing.

I'm so grateful he doesn't care about the scars on my body.

"I guess I can count this as one of my workouts," he says.

"Part of your training. For your fight?"

He nods. Then he sits up, about to get out of bed. I reach and grab his arm. He turns and looks at me.

"Can you stay the night?"

He shrugs. "Really? I'll have to leave early tomorrow morning."

"That's fine. I just don't want to be alone right now."

After so many nights by myself, it's nice to have someone by my side. I want to feel his warm body next to mine as I fall asleep. Even though he's a stranger to me in so many ways, the thought of his presence comforts me.

"What if that paparazzi guy sees me leaving tomorrow morning?"

"I don't care. I need this," I confess. "I mean, you. I need you to spend the night."

"Alright," he says and lies back down. I scoot closer to him and rest my head against his chest. I hear his heart beating under the mass of muscle. I find it soothing. *I'm not alone.*

"You don't mind, do you?"

"No. Not at all," he replies.

I don't know if he's lying, but I want to believe it's true – that right now –there's no other place he'd rather be.

I smell him, and feel him lying next to me. I let out a sigh.

"You all right?" he asks.

I raise my head and look at him. I love his eyes. They hold me captive. Slowly, I nod. "Just thinking…" I confess.

"What?"

"Do you really care?" I ask. Part of me wants to know what is an illusion and what just might be real.

"I wouldn't ask if I wasn't interested," he replies.

"It's stupid, really," I say shaking my head. I

immediately check to make sure my mask hasn't shifted. I hate this mask. But I can't find the courage to take it off. As I look at him again, I allow myself to be completely honest. "I wonder if I'm going to have to pay to spend time with a man for the rest of my life?"

"Because of the mask?" he asks softly.

I nod. "Not just that. My body, too."

"You don't have to worry about your body," he tells me. "I really enjoy fucking you."

"You're just saying that because I'm paying you."

He shakes his head. "You can think that if you want. But it wouldn't be the truth. Sex with you is the best sex I've ever had. You're so passionate, so in the moment."

I look at him. Could he be telling me the truth? Or is this just part of his job, to make me feel special? But the look in his eyes appears so genuine.

"Listen," he continues. "The only way you'll ever be with a man in any meaningful way is if you're comfortable with who you are."

I sigh. "Which means taking off the mask," I reply.

He nods.

"I know." I drop my head onto his chest. "I'm just not ready for that. Not yet," I tell him.

He rubs my shoulder and trails his hand down my arm. His touch is so comforting.

"I can see how it's scary," he says. Then he begins talking, confiding in me. For a man of few words, he's surprisingly candid. "I remember years ago, when I went on my first tour, one of my commanders told me that it's the scared ones that always get killed. Now, I don't think that's true. Because from what I could tell, we were all scared. But I think the point he was trying to make is: fear controls you. It's the fear that kills you, sometimes slowly, sometimes clear out of nowhere. The fear will always be there. But you have to make your peace with it, recognize it and move on, whatever happens."

I raise my head and look at him again. I want to kiss him now more than ever. He understands. "Thank you," I tell him softly.

"For what?"

"For being here."

There's a long pause. I sense he wants to say something, but he hesitates. He just keeps looking at me with those intense, deep, dark eyes.

"Did you start fighting when you came back from the war?" I eventually ask him.

"Yeah."

There's a pause and then he says, "It helped."

"With what?" I ask.

He lets out a big exhale and starts talking again. I hang on every word. Kade captivates me. I want to know everything about him.

"Over there," he begins. "In the Middle East, you know in a second it can all be over. You go from boredom to something exploding, just like that. You can lose your life to a hidden explosive or a ten year-old kid with a gun. The shadow of death is always hanging over you. But when you come back here, it's like you were never gone. Life went on without you. Everybody goes to the mall like it's totally normal. Nothing's changed: But *you* have. It's like you're an alien in your own home. People keep saying our freedom needs to be defended.

But they don't care what happens to the people who are in charge of defending it: The sacrifices they make, physical and mental. I'm one of the lucky ones. I didn't have a bomb blow off my leg or arm. I just came back angry. Fighting in MMA helped me get rid of some of that anger, but when Max…"

He stops.

I want him to continue. *Who is Max?* Is he the boy tattooed on his chest? I want to know more about his life.

I glance at the tattoo of the smiling boy. I run my hand over the child's face.

"Please, don't ask," he says softly.

I glance away from the tattoo and stare at his face once again. I see a whirlwind of emotion swimming in his eyes: pain, grief, anger… I feel instantly drawn to him. Now, it's clear to me that Kade has experienced great loss. I can see the heavy weight of sorrow pulling him down; it's in his eyes. We've both lost something. But his loss is much greater than mine. He lost a child. Nothing I've gone through can compare to that terrifying loss.

I'm overcome with a desire to comfort him, to kiss him. I have to push the urge away. Because the longer it lingers, it will only sadden me.

I lower my head to his chest. I can hear him trying to steady his breathing. He's struggling to regain his composure, fighting to bury those emotions or memories. I know what it's like because I do the same thing.

I decide to change the topic of conversation.

"So, can I see you fight on TV?"

He clears his throat. "No. I fight underground now," he finally says. "I owe a guy a favor. One of the fighters pulled out last minute and he asked me to fill in."

"What's the difference between an underground fight and what I see on TV?"

"No rules. Anything goes."

"Could you get hurt? Like seriously injured?" I ask.

"It can happen. The last fight I broke my leg."

I sit up. "I hope you're getting paid a lot of money for this."

He looks at me, and I can still see the emotional tempest brewing in his eyes. "It's complicated," he finally says. "I owe somebody."

I want to know more but decide not to pry. I lower my head to his chest. His hand slowly rubs my arm again.

"So, what's your album going to be called?" he asks in an attempt to change the mood.

I shrug. "I haven't given it any thought. It probably won't even be released. I just have to record it as part of my contract."

"Then why do you care if the songs are good? Your assistant made it sound like you really care about the music. She said that's why you need to keep seeing me. She said I inspire you."

"Did she really say that?"

"Yeah. So does that make me your muse or something?" he asks, the tone in his voice now lighter.

I shrug and pat his firm chest. "Maybe you are," I reply. If I wasn't wearing my mask, he could see that I'm smiling.

"But seriously," he says. "Why do you care if the songs are good, if you don't even want people to hear them?"

"Because I don't believe in doing shitty work," I tell him.

"I respect that," he replies.

"The irony is," I confide, "Now that I don't have to worry about my career, the music is going in some really cool directions. Ever since we've been fucking, I've written some pretty good stuff."

"Go figure," he says.

"Yeah. Go figure."

Damn, it feels good to be with a man, like this, just talking in bed. I don't want him to leave in the morning.

"But what if the label likes the songs? And wants to release the album," he asks.

"Doesn't matter. They won't want me to tour."

"Why?"

"Because of what I look like underneath this mask. It would be a freak show."

He squeezes my arm tenderly.

"You have too much talent to stay locked up in here," he says.

"My days of performing are over," I mutter.

We fall into silence, my head resting against his chest. I slip into sleep, listening to the beating of his heart.

23

Melody

"How do I look?"

"Like you're going on a hot date?"

"I don't look fat, do I?"

Suzie couldn't look fat even if she tried. It's really annoying. She's wearing a safari emerald green print dress that works perfectly with her red hair.

"No. You look hot as fuck."

"Awesome."

She snaps her clutch shut and walks over to the piano. She moves Mingus and takes a seat on the bench next to me.

"Okay, you were right. I admit it," she says with a shrug.

"About?" I ask.

"It's not Mingus. It's him. The last three songs have been awesome."

"I told you," I say with a smirk. "Kade fucked me out of my stupor."

"I'm worried, though."

"Why?"

Suzie rolls her eyes. "You know this is going to blow

up sooner or later. That jerk was on your lawn trying to get a picture of you. Right now, as we speak, he's parked outside on the street. The press has already gotten pictures of Kade coming over. It's only a matter of time before they find out he's…you know…"

I look at her. "You can say it, Suzie: an escort."

She sighs. "Do you really want to deal with all that, Melody? Does he?"

I ponder her question for a moment. "All I know is that I like being with him," I confess. "I feel comfortable. I feel connected. I haven't felt like this, well honestly, ever. Kade gets me somehow. He gets what I'm going through. I can't explain it. And I know it's fucked up that I'm paying him to have sex with me. But I really don't care what people think right now. I'm happy. That's all that matters. And I'm finally writing music again. Isn't that what everybody wanted: you, Randy, and the label? This is all because of Kade."

Suzie looks at me and softly smiles. She shrugs and gives me a hug. "Okay, I'm just looking out for you."

"I know you are, Suz."

She glances at her phone. "Shit. I'm late." She jumps from the piano bench and hurries out of the living room. "See you tomorrow."

"Have fun with Brian," I shout.

She shouts back from the kitchen, "It's Bradley, Melody. Bradley!"

"Like Bradley Cooper?"

"I wish," Suzie replies as she shuts the door behind her.

I laugh to myself. Mingus returns to his spot on the

piano bench beside me. I rub his back then return to playing with the keys.

An hour passes as I continue searching for a song.

Tonight, I'm having trouble finding a tune. I can't concentrate. I feel tense, worried.

I know why.

It's Saturday night: the night of his fight. I wish I could see him in action. Is he beating the crap out of some guy? Or is he getting hit? He must be winning. I can sense it. He's not holding back in the ring, or the cage, or whatever they call it. He seems like the type that never holds back. He definitely doesn't in the bedroom, that's for sure. I haven't been fucked like this since… well never. He's like an untamed animal in the sack.

What's going on with me? Why can't I stop thinking about him? It's got to be because I haven't been with anyone in such a long time. I'm projecting a bunch of stuff onto Kade. I'm sure that's what my therapist would say, if I hadn't fired her.

I'm projecting. Yeah, that's it.

Kade's an escort for crying out loud. I'm paying him to fuck me. It's a very simple arrangement. So why am I complicating it? Why can't I get him out of my head? I can't stop thinking about him and the fight. Is he getting his leg broken again? Is his face all bloodied? Why do I care?

Mingus begins huffing. I turn and pick him up.

"You're right, Mingus. I just have to put all this into my music. I can't let Kade consume me."

Mingus huffs again. I nod.

"I know. It's going to be tough because he's so

gorgeous. But we're from two different worlds. It would never work between us, except in the movies."

Mingus barks.

I nod again in agreement.

"He is dark and mysterious. It's true."

Mingus licks my hand.

"Okay, enough of that." I place him on the ground. I begin playing with the keys and something slowly begins forming. I follow the energy, see where it goes. Before I know it, I'm muttering some words and a verse begins to emerge.

A few hours later, I'm in my recording studio, singing into the mic. It's a song about him. A song about who he's fighting for – himself and the son he lost.

As I continue singing the words I have jotted on paper, I realize the song is also about me. How I'm not as strong as I thought I was. How I wish I had someone in my corner. Someone who believed in me unconditionally… besides Suzie. I wish I had a man who loved me for who I am now: the bare-boned and fragile me, a woman whose lost her beauty and can't be redeemed by make-up.

When I'm done singing, I put together a rough mix and play it back. The song is raw, stripped down. It's honest. I hear the fear in my voice. It chills me to the core.

Then I think about him and hope he's all right, and not somewhere beaten, bloodied, and on the floor.

24

KADE

I'm kicking ass, and it feels great. Mitch Cork, my opponent, doesn't know what to do. He comes at me with a jab, but I'm too fast. I hit him with a cross then sweep in with a high leg kick, knocking him off balance. He stumbles. Then I unleash a fury of punches. He falls down, and I go full press on the motherfucker, unleashing a ground and pound. The crowd outside the cage erupts. They're cheering me on. Mitch's face is bloodied and swollen.

If this were a professional fight, a referee would have called it by now. But we're in the underground: him and me are going the distance.

I'm surprised Mitch still has some life in him. He thrusts his pelvis forward and hits me with a cross. I roll off him, and we both get to our feet.

We stare each other down, as the crowd around us grows hysterical. These people are bloodthirsty. They want more.

Mitch is breathing heavily. I don't know how much more he has in him. I'm surprised by how good I feel. Sure, I'm exhausted. But I have more in the tank. I surge forward and jump, twisting my body. I hit him square in the jaw with a tornado kick.

Blood spurts out of his mouth as he falls to the floor. He's out cold. Someone rushes into the cage to check on him. After a few moments, Mitch finally opens his eyes. He's all right. But he lost.

The crowd outside the cage cheers. It takes me a moment to realize they're chanting my name. I scan the sea of faces then stop when I see Shane. He's grinning and gives me a nod.

I have a hunch I just made him a lot of money.

25

Melody

It's been three days since the fight. I've thought about calling him to see how it went. Would that be foolish? Then I think about calling him to schedule another meeting. But I realize his body might need some time to recover from the fight. Sure, I'm paying him a lot of money to fuck me when I need it, but I don't want to sound like some commanding bitch.

Recording that song about him has really peaked my interest. I want to get to know Kade on more than just a physical level. I'm drawn to him; I can't deny it. There's just something about him.

The doorbell rings. I put on my mask. As I enter the kitchen, I see Randy and Suzie. Suzie is holding a bottle of champagne. She shoots me a nervous smile.

"What's going on?" I ask them.

"What's going on?" repeats Randy, a smile beaming on her face. "You're a fuckin' genius! That's what's going on."

I glance over at Suzie and notice she's avoiding eye contact with me.

"Thanks for the compliment," I reply, "But why do I

have the sneaking suspicion I might not like the reason behind it?"

Randy turns to Suzie. "Suzie, pop that champagne and pour three glasses, please. We need to celebrate."

I approach Randy, suspicious. "What exactly are we celebrating?"

Randy claps her hands ecstatically. "The label *loves* your new songs, especially the last one about the fighter. They want to start dropping them ASAP."

A loud pop echoes throughout the kitchen. Suzie pours three glasses of champagne.

"But that's not the best part," continues Randy.

Suzie hands me my glass and whispers, "I just found out, Melody. You're not going to like it."

"Found out what?" I ask, now getting worried.

"They want to schedule a tour for this summer!" says Randy. She's super excited.

My heart catches in my throat. I couldn't have heard her correctly.

"What?"

Randy nods, her smile still beaming. "I know. Amazing, isn't it? The label believes this could be the comeback of the century. They want to pull out all the stops. They don't even want to wait until the album is ready."

"Nobody cares about albums anymore," says Suzie with a sad shrug.

"It's true," concurs Randy. "They want to release the songs as you write them. Do some music videos."

"Music videos," I repeat, my head spinning. Nervous tension ricochets through my body.

"Definitely one for that last song you wrote. That song is hot," says Randy.

"It's really good," mutters Suzie. "I cried when I heard it. It's your best song yet."

I look at the two of them, shocked.

"This can't be happening?" I say, lowering my head.

"I know, it's incredible," exclaims Randy. "After everything you've been through, you're still going to be on top. You're going back on tour!"

I look at Randy and see her staring at me, excited. I throw my glass of champagne straight at her face.

"Melody, what's wrong with you?" she shouts.

"I'm not going out there. I'm not going on tour!" I cry.

I hurry out of the kitchen. The two of them follow me into the living room.

"I don't understand," says Randy. "This is great news."

I whirl around. "How is this great news, Randy?"

"People still want to hear what you have to say. Don't you realize how lucky you are?"

She clearly doesn't realize the horrific panic I'm in.

I beat my fists into my legs, bend forward and scream.

"I want people to stop telling me how lucky I am! If I'm so lucky, then trade places with me. Would you do that, Randy? Would you put yourself out there and get every aspect of your appearance scrutinized? Deal with all the haters online commenting on how ugly you are?! Listen to them talk about your fuckin' ugly face?! I'm the one who has to deal with that. Me. Not you. It's easy to say I'm lucky when you get to watch me from the sidelines. You're not the one standing in the burning white spotlight."

I'm out of breath, exhausted. I take a seat on the couch. Randy and Suzie stare at me in silence. Randy wipes the champagne off her face with a towel.

"I'm sorry, Randy," I mutter. "I shouldn't have done that."

"No, you shouldn't have," she replies. With a sigh she adds, "But I understand. Although you might not believe it, Melody, I do care about you. Yes, it's true I work for you; but that's not the only reason I'm here. I'm not like your mom and dad. I want to see you happy. You may not want to admit it, but you won't be truly happy until you're able to face the world again. We both know you can't stop singing and writing songs. It's in your blood. And what good is it to write such amazing music if nobody is ever going to hear it or see you perform?"

"I can't go on tour. I'm not ready," I plead looking up at her.

Mingus suddenly jumps on my lap. I rub his belly. Then, Randy takes a seat on the couch next to me.

"I just need more time, Randy. I can't go out there yet. I'm scared. I just need more time"

Randy nods. "I know it's not going to be easy."

I can tell by the look in her eyes that there's something else she wants to say, but she's wavering. I turn to Suzie. She's staring at the ground, and avoids looking at me.

"What is it? There's something else, isn't there?"

Randy finally manages to get it out. "I hate telling you this. Especially since I know you might not be ready. But based on the contract you have with the label, if they like the album, they can require you tour in a minimum of twelve markets."

My jaw drops. "They can force me to go on tour?"

Randy closes her eyes and nods. "If you refuse to tour this summer, they can claim you're in breach of contract and sue."

"I have the label from fuckin' hell, Randy! Why on earth would we ever agree to that?!"

Carrying Mingus in my arms, I angrily get up from the couch. I head to the window and look out, onto my backyard.

"It was part of the renegotiation we made four years ago with the label," says Randy. "Unless you want to be dragged into court, I'm afraid you have no choice but to tour."

"I can't believe this," I complain.

"Melody, I know you might not want to hear this," says Suzie. "But I don't think everyone is going to be mean to you. Sure, there are going to be some assholes, but just ignore them. People loved you before the accident, and when they hear these new songs, they're going to love you again."

I know Suzie means well, but I've stopped listening as she continues talking. I just stare out my window in a daze. I'm going to have to face the world.

I'm not ready.

I'm scared out of my mind.

26

KADE

Four days after the fight and I'm still sore in a million different places. Although my body aches, I must admit I'm happy. Melody wired the hundred thousand into my account before the fight. And after my victory in the octagon, I'm a bit of a hero at the gym. I guess Shane was right. There still are some fighting years in me. I'm about to lie down in bed, try to catch some sleep, when my cell phone rings. It's her.

"How are you?" she asks. I can tell by the tone in her voice that she's rattled, nervous.

"I'm good. You?"

"I wanted to call you but didn't want to bother you, in case you were recovering. How'd you do… in the fight?"

"I won."

"Congratulations." There's a long pause. "Can I see you… tonight?"

I slowly sit up in bed. My body needs some rest, but I can hear the desperation in her voice. "Yeah, sure."

"Thank you," she replies.

The way she sounds makes me realize tonight may not be about sex.

"No worries. I'll see you in a bit."

I hang up and get dressed.

When I arrive at her place – even though I can't see her face – I can tell by her body language that she's a nervous wreck. She offers me a beer, which I take. Then, we walk into the living room.

She heads to the bay window that overlooks her backyard. She stares into the night. Mingus, the puppy, is at my heels. I scoop him up with one hand and let him rest in the crook of my arm. I take a swig from my beer.

"What's up?" I ask.

She slowly turns around. She stares at me through the eyeholes in her mask.

"What's up… Is that I wish I never met you."

Shit. Does she want to cancel our arrangement? I thought we had a good thing going. Did I do something wrong? Does she want the hundred grand she wired into my account back?

"Why?" is the only word I manage to mutter.

She sighs. She steps toward a laptop resting on the grand piano. "Because of this," she says as she presses a button. A song begins playing through the speakers.

You rob my gut
Of all that I got
Take away my smile

My blood, my tears
My youth, my years
They've all disappeared

But I'm fighter in a cage
A tiger filled with rage
The battle has been staged

She takes a seat on the piano stool. We're both silent as her voice echoes through the room. It's a slow, sad song. Raw and intense. I listen to the lyrics and realize the song is about me. About me being a fighter. But when the chorus kicks in and the next verse plays, I realize the song is about much more. It's like she stared into my soul and put into words every thing I've been struggling with. But how? I look at her in disbelief as the song continues.

I'll never give up
I won't break for you
You'll have to kill me you fool

But you still want more
Turn me into a whore
I can't settle this score

My heart's gone numb
There's only empty space
Where love's memory took place

Suddenly, anguish overwhelms me. I'm being attacked from the inside. I picture Max, staring at me from the hospital bed. His eyes almost lifeless. Tears run down my face. *Fuck*. I'm crying. Right here, in front of her. I wipe away the tears with the back of my hand. I bend down and lower Mingus to the floor. I lean against the wall and close my eyes as the song continues.

> *Maybe I'll meet you again*
> *Up the stairs at heaven's end*
> *Until then, farewell, my friend*

I want to shove the emotion creeping up my throat back down, but I can't. There's something about her voice, the way it sounds, her words.

Fuck, I'm still crying. I can't stop.

l drop to the floor, squat, and lower my head. I put the beer down.

> *But until that day*
> *I'll fight and I'll pray*
> *I'll fight and I'll pray*
> *Until the pain goes away*

The song ends.
Silence fills the space between us.

27

Melody

He's like a wounded animal, crouching on the floor before me. He's embarrassed, ashamed of this uncontrollable show of emotion. I've never seen someone break like this in front of me. I feel terrible. I *knew* he was haunted by loss. But I never thought my music could take him to such a painful place. Seeing this strong fighter crumble in my presence, when reminded of his son, brings me to tears.

I've been selfish. I didn't consider the impact the song might have on him. I asked him to come over so he could comfort me, because I was frightened by the thought of going on tour. But now, I realize he is the one who needs comforting. I've been obsessed with my own problems, my own fears, my own anger, and my own insecurities. I didn't realize the depth of his loss. Sure, I could understand it in the abstract. But to actually go through something like that… losing your child… that's unimaginable.

I wish I never wrote this song.

I need to apologize. But words aren't enough. I want to comfort him somehow. I want to kiss him.

Then slowly, I realize what I need to do.

I reach behind my head and loosen my mask. He's still looking at the ground, avoiding my gaze. He's struggling to find composure.

My hands trembling, I slowly slip the mask off, revealing my face.

He will be *the one*. The first, to see me as I truly am.

I want him to know that seeing his pain has given me the strength to move forward. I want him to know how grateful I am that he's helped me.

Having him see me, without my mask, is the only gesture that makes sense.

I take a few steps forward. He's still hiding his face.

My body is shaking with nerves.

"I'm sorry," I say, my voice quivering. "For what happened. I'm so sorry. I didn't mean for my song to…" I can't finish the sentence. Words are inadequate.

My fingers tremble as I clutch the mask in my hands.

28

KADE

I can't look at her. I don't want her to see me like this. I'm a pussy. A fuckin' mess.

There's a long silence. I hear her footsteps getting closer. She's standing over me.

"I'm so sorry," she says softly. "For what happened. I'm so sorry. I didn't mean for my song to…"

I nod my head slowly. "It's okay," I mumble. I can hear the weakness in my voice. I still can't look her in the eyes. I keep my head low and stare at the floor. I'm almost sick by how weak I am right now. I can't be weak. I have to be strong. I have to move forward. I have to live the life Max never got the chance too.

When I finally look up, I see something white in my line of sight. It's her mask. She's holding it in her trembling hand.

Stunned, I look up.

I can see her face.

Slowly, I rise.

She looks straight at me, her face exposed. I explore her scar-pulled skin, the discoloration.

In shock, I look into her eyes. I don't know what to

say. Just seconds ago, I was in the midst of an emotional storm thinking about Max. Now, I'm standing in awe of her courage.

"You're the reason I can finally do this," she says, her voice shaking.

I step forward and gently run my hand over her cheek.

"It's pretty bad, isn't it?" she asks, looking distressed.

I slowly shake my head. There are no words for a moment like this.

I lean forward and kiss her.

I dip my tongue into her warm mouth. Our tongues come together in a dance.

"You taste good," she says in between kisses.

I wrap my arms around her and embrace her tightly.

"Thank you," I tell her.

"For what?" she asks, confused.

"Just thank you," I reply.

When I look at her, I notice her eyes are filled with tears. We kiss again. The kisses grow more passionate. And soon, kisses aren't enough. I yank off my t-shirt and she presses her hands against my chest. I reach for her skirt, lift it and pull down her panties.

I tug on her bottom lip and growl. "I need you… now."

"Take me," she breathes, as she presses her lips against mine.

There's no time for the bedroom. I want to get inside her at once. I feel intrinsic, unbridled passion for her. I lower her to the floor and slip her undies off her feet. Quickly unzipping my fly, I yank out my cock. I'm already hard, desperately craving her.

She reaches and tugs on my shaft. She guides it toward the voice between her legs.

As we lie on her living room floor, staring deeply into each other's eyes, I slide my cock inside her.

She tilts her head back with a groan. A smile spreads over her face. I thank God that mask is finally off. I lean forward and kiss her again.

As I grind my hips against hers, driving my cock in deeper, she moans with pleasure. She wraps her legs around me and grabs my ass.

She dips her tongue into my mouth and grins.

"I've wanted to kiss you for so long," she says, breathlessly.

The heat between us intensifies. Our bodies meld, our tongues dance. We let go together. And when we come, we come together. Both of us groan into each other's ears. After we orgasm, we just lie still, staring at each other.

I gently touch her face.

"Why now?" I ask.

She shrugs and rests her head against my shoulder. "I don't know what came over me," she confesses. "When I saw you crying in front of me, I realized you were vulnerable. You looked so alone, in so much pain. I know what that feels like. I wanted you to know that you weren't alone. I felt an urge to comfort you. To kiss you. The mask was in the way. So, without really thinking, I took it off. You kissed me first though. That was a surprise."

"I can't believe I cried like that. I'm such a pussy," I mutter.

"Grown men cry, Kade. It's good to let out your emotions," she says.

I look at her and grin. Then I kiss her one more time.

As our lips part, she looks at me and sighs.

"That song," she says. "I wrote it the night you were at the fight. My label released it today. It hit number one."

I'm surprised by the defeated look on her face.

"Most people would be happy about a thing like that," I say.

She looks at me, her face filled with worry. "They want me to tour this summer, Kade. I'm petrified. People are going to be so cruel," she fears. "When they see me, looking like this."

"Fuck them," I tell her. "You can take it."

"You make it sound easy."

"Not at all. Every day will be a battle. But you're a fighter."

She shakes her head. "I'm not like you."

"Yes, you are," I tell her. "That's why when we fuck, it's so amazing. We've got the same spirit. We just got the shit kicked out of us for a bit. We both lost our way. But you've got a gift, Melody. You're still here so you can share it with the world."

"So, it's now or never, you're basically telling me."

I shrug. "There's never going to be a good time. Just like there's never enough time to train for a fight. You just have to get in there and slug it out. But I don't need to tell you any of this. You just wrote a song about it."

"You know the only good thing that came from my accident?" she whispers.

"What?" I ask.

"I met you."

As I pull her closer to me, I'm filled with a sense of gratitude. I'm happy to be here, with her.

29

KADE

I'm standing outside the octagon in my gym, watching Luke spar with that kid, Rico. But my mind is elsewhere. It's focused on her. I can't stop thinking about Melody, about last night. We bared our souls to each other. Lying on her living room floor, I told her about Max, about his illness, how my life fell apart after he died. I told her about Shane, how he paid for Max's treatment. But in exchange, he hires me out through his website, and now he owns my gym. I told her everything… even how close I came to killing myself. Melody just listened and let me speak. I got it all off my chest. It was such a relief to finally share this burden with someone else. To tell someone all the shit I've been feeling.

Last night, I was more honest with Melody than I've ever been with another human being.

I hear a loud thud. Luke has thrown Rico to the mat.

"Guys, take a break," I shout.

They both look at me and nod. In all honesty, it's me who needs a break: a break from thinking about her.

I head to my office to go over some paperwork. As I plop down in my chair, I hear Shane say, "Damn, this place is getting crowded."

I turn and see him standing in the doorway. His two goons, Vince and Leo, are behind him.

"We've had a couple of new people join this week," I tell him.

"Because they heard about your beat down?"

I shrug. "Maybe."

Shane walks into the office with a grin. He hands me his phone.

"Have you seen this?"

I glance at the screen and watch a video clip of my tornado kick knocking out Mitch Cork. It's my first time seeing it. I gotta admit: it's a work of beauty.

"He was out before he hit the floor," Shane says.

I hand him back his phone. "I had a moment."

"Yeah, you fuckin' had a moment. That shit was legend, Kade."

"Like you said, maybe there's still some fight in me."

Shane takes a seat opposite my desk. He looks around my office. Although technically, it's his office... for now.

"Well, now that the fight is over, I want to get you back on the site."

"About that," I say. "I can't do the site any more."

I see Shane's relaxed manner change. His face hardens.

"That's not how this works, Kade."

"If you want me to pay you back all your money, I can't go back on the site."

Shane leans back, confused. "What the fuck are you talking about?"

I slide open my desk drawer and remove an envelope. I toss it at him. His eyes widen as he looks inside and sees the wad of hundred dollar bills.

"There's more," I tell him. "I just can't take it all out of my bank account. Something about withdrawal limits. I need to wire it to you or something."

Shane stares at me like he wants to kiss me. Like I said, there's nothing he loves more than money.

"How much we talking?"

I shrug. "Probably enough to pay back all I owe you in the next few months. My last client, she's somebody famous. She took a liking to me; and she wants to put me on retainer. She's paying me two hundred thousand a month to help her out. I didn't want to mention it until I knew the deal was legit and the money was for real."

He stares at me, still shocked.

"Two hundred Gs? A month?"

I nod.

His face gets deadly serious. He leans forward. "Kade," he says slowly, in a low tone. "I ain't gay. But if I ever try it, you've got to be the one who fucks me, because that cock of yours must be magical. It's the gift that just keeps on fuckin' giving." He grins then stands up. "Fuck me, this is going to be a good month!" he shouts.

It's been a long time since I've seen Shane this happy. I glance at Vince and Leo, who are standing outside my office. For a split second, I catch an expression of surprise on their faces.

Shane closes the door on them. He walks over to me, puts his hands down on the desk and stares me straight in the eyes. He's got a wide, toothy grin plastered across his face.

"I swear to God I want to kiss you right now," he says.

"You know, for a guy who says he's not gay, there's a lot of subtext going on here."

Shane ignores my comment. He sits back down and takes a deep breath.

I swear, I think he just came in his pants thinking about all the money he's about to receive.

"You know what the best part of all this is?" he says.

I shake my head.

He looks at me, his expression now serious. "You're going to make me even more money with something I got planned. And by the end of the month, you'll have your debt all paid up. You won't owe me a single cent."

I can't believe what I'm hearing. It feels like I'm getting let out of jail early.

"What you talking about?"

Shane leans back in his chair, relaxed, like a man who has it all figured out.

"Your fight with that Irish dude. It made me a lot of money, Kade. Everybody's talking about it. You've built up quite a reputation. People want to see you fight again. They remember when you broke your leg because you wouldn't tap out. And now that you beat that Irish mick, well, word out on the street is that you're the second coming."

I hold up my hands and shake my head. "I got lucky this time. I was in the zone. I can't fight again without proper training time. I need more than a week's notice."

Shane nods. "I hear ya. But what I'm saying is… I think I can build up the next fight. Make it a big purse."

"Okay," I say with a shrug.

Shane leans in. "I think most people will be betting on you to win. Odds will be in your favor."

I see the glimmer in his eyes. I'm suspicious, and then it hits me.

"I ain't never thrown a fight, Shane."

He leans back in his chair. "Well, there's always a first time. Isn't there?"

I can't stomach the thought of it. Losing on purpose goes against everything I believe in. The cage is my church. It's sacrilege to throw a fight.

"Kade, you know what the difference between you and me is?"

I look at Shane, sickened by his proposal.

"You don't see the big picture," he says. "I bet against you on this next fight, and you throw it: Your debt with me is wiped clean. You're a free man."

"I can't do it, Shane."

No matter how much I want my freedom, there are certain lines I can't cross.

He gets up from his chair. "There ain't no such thing as a moral victory, Kade. You should know that by now. There's just money. It makes the world go round. Those who have it, get the opportunities. Those who don't, end up somebody's bitch."

I shake my head. "I can't throw a fight."

Shane looks pissed. He's used to getting his way. He takes a deep breath and sighs. After a moment of contemplation, he speaks.

"How about this? You throw this fight, not only is your debt squared with me, but I'll also let you get your gym back."

I look at him in disbelief. He knows how much this place means to me. I built it from scratch years ago. Now that Max is gone, the gym is the only thing I have left that I'm proud of. It kills me that I no longer own it.

And now Shane is using it as leverage.

He's about to open the door and walk out but stops himself. He turns to me and says, "Don't let your pride get in the way, Kade. Especially after everything you've been through. Throw the fight and the gym is yours."

Then he leaves.

30

Melody

It's 1 am. I can't sleep. Two days ago, I had my final round of plastic surgery. Now I'm staring at my reflection in the mirror. The swelling has gone down. I'm meeting with a special make-up person later this week to learn how to properly blend the various skin tones on my face. No matter how good the make-up job, I'll never resemble my old self. I have to accept I *never* will. The disfigured face staring back at me in the mirror belongs to me. It's not going anywhere. It's who I am now.

After taking my mask off in front of Kade, I'm slowly accepting that reality.

That being said, the thought of standing on stage and having people take pictures of me still fills me with dread. As I envision the experience, my body tenses. I take several deep breaths to prevent another panic attack.

I look at my feet, expecting to see Mingus. I want to cuddle him in my arms, feel his comfort and unconditional love. He's not there. I get up, leave my bedroom and search the house. I call his name; no response.

"Mingus!"

Still no response.

Strange…

Suddenly, I panic. My heart races. My hands go numb. Did he runaway? Did he sneak out of the house and get hit by a car?

I search every room and thankfully find him cuddled into a ball behind a couch.

"There you are," I say with relief. But I notice something isn't right. Mingus is quiet. His eyes are glassy. Then I notice the vomit on the floor.

I nervously pick him up. His breathing is scant and his belly is swollen. What do I do? I run and grab my cellphone from the kitchen counter. I call Suzie. I need her to take Mingus to the vet. But the call goes straight to voicemail. Where the fuck is she? It's 1 am! If she's sleeping, wake-up! I call Randy, again voicemail. Nobody's answering! I need someone to drive Mingus to the vet ASAP! He's not well and he needs immediate attention. I consider calling Kade but then realize he lives too far away. I need to get Mingus help now!

I hear the little dog wheeze. Shit, he really doesn't look good.

I don't want him to die.

I can't let that happen.

I have to drive him to the vet myself.

I quickly search my phone for the nearest animal hospital. There's a place fifteen minutes away. As I leave the house with Mingus, I catch my reflection in the hallway mirror. I'm not wearing my mask. I'm not ready to have anyone, other than Kade, see me without it. I quickly throw it on and leave.

I haven't driven a car since the accident. Jitters crawl up my spine. As I step inside my car, my heart is pounding. I'm having flashbacks to the night of the accident – that truck flying out of nowhere, the shattered glass. I try to shake the images away. I need to get Mingus help. I have to push through this fear. With my trembling hand, I insert the key into the ignition and start my car. I glance at the passenger seat. Mingus looks like he's knocking on heaven's door. "You're going to be okay, buddy."

Mingus doesn't whimper a reply. I only hear him wheeze.

Filled with worry, I pull my car into the street. I begin following the directions from the GPS to the animal hospital.

In my rearview mirror, I see a red Volkswagen bug following me. It's Charlie. Fuck, not again. It's just like the night of the accident. My trembling hands clutch the steering wheel. My breaths are short and quick. I don't know if I can do this.

Then I hear Mingus whimper in the passenger seat. This isn't about me. It's about him.

I need to get Mingus help.

I take a deep breath and continue following the GPS directions. As I drive, I keep glancing at Mingus. I place a hand on his nose; it's hot and dry.

"Just hold on buddy. We'll get you fixed up, I promise."

The GPS directs me to make a left turn. When I glance in my rearview mirror, Charlie is still following me. I can't waste any time by trying to lose him. I need to get Mingus help immediately.

Luckily, there's no traffic on the way to the animal hospital. Within fifteen minutes, I'm slamming my car door shut, and cradling Mingus in my arms. I rush through the clinic's front door.

I must look quite a sight, wearing my mask and pajamas, carrying my poor puppy in my arms. But I don't care. I just want someone to tell me Mingus is going to be okay.

The guy working the front desk says the vet can see Mingus immediately.

Thank God.

"He's not himself. He vomited. His belly is bloated," I nervously tell the vet as I carry him into the room.

The vet, an older lady, looks at me and offers a comforting smile. "Let's take a look. He's in safe hands now. You can calm down, Miss?"

"Swanson," I reply. When she tells me to calm down, I realize how hysterical I've been. I can't lose Mingus. I love the little guy.

The vet ponders my last name, and her eyes light up. She's put two and two together… my mask plus my last name. She realizes who I am. I'm grateful that she doesn't say anything. The last thing I want to discuss right now is who I am and deal with questions about my accident. We need to focus on getting Mingus back to normal.

After a thorough inspection, the vet informs me that Mingus has something lodged in his throat.

"Really? How could I not have known?" I reply, angry

with myself.

"It happens. Puppies tend to chew on anything," she explains. "Sometimes they snatch something up they shouldn't have. We're going to have to sedate him, but I think we'll be able to remove it."

I watch, worried, as the vet and her assistant sedate Mingus. Then I'm shocked when the vet removes a chewed up tube sock from Mingus's throat. "Here's the culprit," she says with a smile. "We were lucky you brought him in when you did. We didn't have to perform surgery. We got it before it hit the gastrointestinal tract. He should be okay, now. Just give him some time to wake up."

"Thank god," I cry. "Thank you so much. I can't thank you enough."

The vet and her assistant smile and exchange glances. Once her assistant leaves the room, I notice the vet staring at me. I can sense what's coming.

"If it isn't too much bother," she says, "Would you mind if I took a selfie with you? My daughter is one of your biggest fans."

I touch my mask. I used to take selfies with strangers all the time. But now, the thought of my image circulating online sends chills down my spine. I shake my head. "I'm sorry. After the accident, I don't take selfies anymore."

The vet nods, clearly disappointed. I feel bad, especially since she just saved Mingus's life.

"If you want, I can write your daughter a letter and sign it."

The vet perks up. "She would love that. Thank you so

much."

"Not a problem."

The vet's assistant enters the room. She looks at me with some hesitation. "Miss Swanson, I think you should know that there are a lot of reporters outside."

I was expecting Charlie to be waiting for me in the parking lot, but a lot of reporters? How did they get tipped off? Then I realize anyone working at the clinic might have sent a tweet. A tweet can go viral in seconds. What am I going to do? The thought of navigating through a crowd of reporters asking me questions, shoving their cameras in my face, sounds like a nightmare. Shit, I feel a panic attack coming on.

"Excuse me," I say to the vet and her assistant.

I step into the hallway and take several deep breaths.

I can't face the reporters alone. I'm so frightened. I need help. I reach for my cell phone. Suzie and Randy are still not answering. I know he's far away, but I need him. I quickly dial Kade's number. I'm so grateful when he answers.

"Hello."

"I need your help," I blurt into the phone.

He must sense the nervous tension in my voice because he quickly responds, "I'll be right there."

I tell him I'm not home and that I'm at the animal clinic. I give him the address, and he says he's on his way.

When I hang up, I feel a sense of relief. I'm not alone. I have Kade. I walk back into the room and see Mingus slowly moving his legs.

"When will he be okay to leave?" I ask the vet.

She shrugs. "He should be fully awake and alert in

thirty minutes."

"Great," I reply. "I have another question. Is there a back entrance to this place? A way I can get out of here without going through the front and dealing with all those cameras?"

"Sure," says the vet.

"Thank God," I reply.

While Mingus is slowly waking up, I write a letter to the vet's daughter, Amy. Then I call Kade and tell him to park his car in the back of the clinic. When Kade shows up forty-five minutes later, Mingus is fully awake and running around like nothing has happened.

I can't hide how happy I am… Mingus is okay, and Kade is here.

"Thank you so much for coming," I tell him as he walks in the room.

"No worries," he replies with a smile.

Kade gives Mingus a soft pat on the head and asks, "He okay?"

I nod, still grateful.

Kade looks at me and I instantly feel safe. "You ready?" he asks.

Using the back door, Kade quickly walks Mingus and me to his car, a really beat up Toyota Corolla.

As we pull out of the back alley of the clinic, Kade apologizes for the car. "I know it's a piece of shit."

"There's no need to apologize," I tell him. "Right now, it's a chariot whisking me away from all this madness."

He pats the dashboard of his car. "Did you hear that? You're a chariot." Then he looks at me. "You alright?"

I nod, as I look down at Mingus and give him a kiss on

the head. "I really freaked out back there."

"Well, it's all good now. Mingus is back to normal, and you avoided the sharks."

I hold Mingus up and give him a scolding look. "No more socks for you, buddy." He licks my mask without a care in the world. I laugh. I'm so happy he's all right.

"That's the first time I've heard you really laugh," Kade remarks.

"It's been a while," I reply. I glance at him. As I watch the passing car lights highlight his face, I admire how arrestingly handsome he is. He catches me looking and smirks.

"You realize what you did?"

I shake my head. "What?"

"You left your house, all on your own."

It takes me a moment to process it all. It happened so fast. I was so worried about Mingus that I stopped being paralyzed by the outside world.

"You're still wearing the mask, though" Kade remarks.

I sigh. "Kade, the other night with you was a big step. I'm not ready for the whole world to see me, not yet."

"Okay," he says with a shrug. "Baby steps."

"That's right," I tell him.

He reaches to turn on the radio. A song by Adele is playing. Her strong voice fills the night. The neon city lights of Los Angeles pass us by. With my arm dangling outside the car window, I feel the cool breeze against my skin. Then we pass a Mexican restaurant, and I inhale, savoring the aroma of good food. I look at the stars in the sky. I've been a prisoner in my house for so long; I've forgotten how vibrant LA is. I've forgotten what the city's beating heart sounds like. I miss it.

When Adele's song finishes, it's followed by another song... one of mine. One of the new ones. I immediately switch off the radio.

Kade shrugs and looks at me. "Pretty weird, huh? Hearing your voice on the radio."

"I should be happy that it's getting radio play. But right now, I just want to forget who I am." Then I ask him, "Do you think we can go somewhere for a bit? I really don't feel like going home, not yet. My property is probably swarming with reporters."

Kade mulls over the possibilities. "I don't want to take you to my place," he says. "It's a shit hole." He shrugs, then looks at me and smirks. "You want to check out my gym? It's the middle of the night so no one's there."

"Sure."

"Welcome to Kade's Cage," he says with a smile. He unlocks the front door and turns on the lights. The space is larger than I expected. I'm surprised to see it's equipped with an octagon-fighting cage and a boxing ring in the far back.

"I'm impressed," I tell him. "This is a serious gym."

"It's my pride and joy," he replies. And I can tell by the look on his face, as he scans the room, that he's not lying. "We've got everything you might need. If this gym were in a better part of town, it would probably be a huge success. But I'm not complaining. We keep adding new clients every month."

As we walk around, I decide to let Mingus stretch his legs. I lower him to the floor and he takes off, exploring every corner of the gym. "Mingus, don't eat anything!" I shout at him.

He yelps a reply.

"If you're going to go on tour, don't you have to start training? Get your body in shape?" Kade asks.

I shrug. "For half my songs, I sit at the piano. I'm not like Beyoncé. I don't have all these intricate dance routines." Then I realize something. I put my hands on my hips. "Hey, are you saying you don't think I'm in shape?"

Kade holds up his hands in defense and smirks. "Hey, I dig your body, Melody. But if I could have my way with you, I'd get you so lean and mean. You'd be one hot, kick ass beauty."

"I like the way that sounds," I admit.

He approaches me and takes my hands, moving in closer. "I'd get that body of yours so strong, so flexible, that during sex, we'd be able to really go the distance. If you know what I mean."

"Now, that's the best pitch for personal fitness I've ever heard."

He laughs.

We continue walking around. "How long have you had this place?"

"A couple of years." His expression changes. The sense of pride is replaced by regret. "I don't own it anymore, though. Like I told you the other night, I signed it over to Shane in exchange for money to pay for Max's medical bills. I just manage it now."

His disappointment is palpable.

"I still love this place, though," he says with a sigh. As he looks around, he admits, "The war really fucked me up in the head. This place and that cage," he points to the octagon at the end of the gym, "helped me channel all that anger – all the shit that comes with PTSD –into something more constructive. I guess you can say the cage saved me."

"Like my music saved me."

He looks at me and smirks. "Yeah. Same thing."

We walk toward the cage and step inside. I notice the eight fenced walls surrounding us.

"Do you think you can ever get the gym back?" I ask him.

"There might be a chance," he confides. His mood changes again. A dark cloud comes over him.

"What's wrong?"

He looks at me. I sense he wants to tell me something, but then shakes his head. "Nothing. I just have a decision to make," he mumbles.

There's a long silence and I can see the tension in his body, around his neck. It must be about getting his gym back, which involves Shane. But Kade doesn't want to divulge anything more.

"Kade?" I say. He looks at me and I can see the strain in his eyes.

He shakes his head. "Forget it. It's something I need to deal with. It's not a big deal." He looks at the ground, avoiding my gaze.

It obviously *is* a big deal, but he doesn't want to tell me. In order to lighten the mood, I change the topic of conversation.

"So, do you really think you could get me lean and mean?"

He looks up. His face softens. He nods with a smirk. "Most definitely." A curious expression fills his eyes. "In fact, why don't we start now?"

"A workout?"

He shrugs. "Why not? You don't want to go home because of all the paparazzi. We have the gym all to ourselves with some time to kill. Why not get a workout in?"

He's serious.

"Look at me," I say pointing to my pajamas. "I'm not dressed for a workout."

"Who said you needed to be dressed?" Kade replies with a grin.

He steps toward me. Slowly, he begins unbuttoning my pajama top. He slips it off my shoulders, exposing my breasts. He takes his hands and cups my breasts, giving them a firm squeeze. With an appreciative growl, he remarks, "I love your tits."

"I love your hands on them," I admit.

He kneels down and slides my pajama pants over my hips. I kick off my flip-flops. He tosses my pajama bottoms to the side. All that remains is my underwear. Kade moves in closer and grabs my ass. He leans in, pressing his nose against my crotch. Then, he looks up at me. "You know what I love more than your tits, Melody?"

"What?" I ask my voice filled with desire.

"The taste of your cunt. And it's smell."

He presses his nose against my panties and inhales. He curls his fingers over the waistband and slides them down, exposing my sex. I'm so turned on. Before I know it, Kade's tongue presses against my lips. My pussy welcomes the pleasure he's set off. I press the back of his head further into me.

I can't believe it. I'm in an empty gym, standing in the center of an octagon. The hottest man on earth is kneeling before me, licking my most prized possession. I definitely never thought I'd be here.

I'm so turned on. I can't wait to replace his mouth with his cock. Kade stops working magic with his tongue. He glances at me then stands up.

He looks into my eyes as he wipes some of my pussy juice from his lips.

"You know what I want more than anything, Melody?"

"What?"

"To kiss you," he says. "May I?"

He looks deeply into my eyes and I see his compassion.

I slowly nod.

I reach behind my head and loosen my mask. Kade gently lifts it off.

He drops it to the floor. He tenderly holds my face with both of his hands. He leans forward and kisses me. He slips his delicious tongue into my mouth.

After relishing his kiss, I ask, "You know what the best part of taking off this mask is?"

Kade slowly shakes his head.

"Now, I can finally suck on your cock."

He smirks with pleasure.

I glide my hand down his broad, muscular chest. Slowly, I slide it over the bulge in his pants. Through the fabric of his sweatpants, I give his manhood a squeeze. It's incredible how comfortable I am in Kade's presence. It's hard to believe I'm standing naked in his gym, with my mask off. And now, finally, I'm going to be able to suck on that gorgeous cock of his. I slide my hand under the waistband and grab his semi-hard shaft. I pull from the base all the way to the tip and feel it jump to life. As it gets hard in my hand, Kade releases an appreciative moan.

"I can't wait to wrap my lips around it," I confess. I give Kade's luscious lips one last kiss before dropping to my knees. Now it's his turn to be pleasured. I pull his sweatpants down.

I open my mouth and lean forward, wanting to take in his impressive shaft. I clasp his balls and swirl my tongue over the tip of his cock. Then I begin to slowly take him in. I love having his hard shaft in my mouth. I open wide relaxing my throat. As I slowly pull up with my mouth, my hand grips his shaft tightly. When I reach the tip, I go down again, and then up, finding a steady pace.

"God damn, your good with your mouth," Kade moans. "Thank God you took off that mask."

I pull back and catch my breath. I look into his eyes then take him once again. Kade's groans grow louder as I bob my head, sucking and lathering his manhood. My pussy is drenched.

"Fuck that's good," Kade growls.

I increase the pace. I've missed having a cock in my

mouth. And I've wanted his since the first time I saw it.

After I give his cock one good, long suck, I pull my head back and run my tongue over the tip of his shaft. I look at him and simper.

"Kade?"

His face is flush. I can tell he thoroughly enjoyed my blow-job.

"What?" he asks breathlessly.

"Will you please fuck me, now?"

With a rumble, Kade strips off his sweatpants and shirt. He kicks off his sneakers. He yanks me onto my feet and presses his body against mine. We stumble backwards. My back collides with the fenced wall of the cage. Kade leans in and passionately kisses me.

Then he pulls his head back and looks at me.

"I want you so fuckin' badly," he growls.

The way he stares at me makes me feel like there's nothing wrong with my face or my body. Then his passion is suddenly interrupted by a moment of tenderness. He gently slides a strand of my long brown hair behind my ear. He smirks and then shifts forward. I feel the head of his cock press against my crotch.

"It's about time," I say with a smile.

He leans forward and kisses me.

Then he slides himself inside me. I wrap my arms around him and welcome his girth. As he stretches me wide, I whisper into his ear, "I've never been fucked in a cage before. I think I like it."

He lets out another growl and says, "Where have you been all my life?"

31

Melody

"I'm so sorry," says Suzie as she rubs Mingus's head. We're sitting on my living room couch. *Family Feud* is playing on the television. "I should've been paying attention to my phone," she says, apologizing. "I slept at Bradley's place last night. It was our third date. And you know how I like to have sex by the third date to know if the relationship is going anywhere."

"And?" I ask.

Suzie lets out a sigh. "It looks like our third date will be our last," she says with disappointment. "Bradley's really hot. But when we went back to his place and had sex, he was checking out his abs in the full-length mirror in his room the entire time. I can't date someone whose that in love with himself. Anyway, you must've called when we were in the middle of you know… fucking."

It looks like I wasn't the only one having sex last night. Although, based on Suzie's account, I at least enjoyed my experience. I'm still surprised that Kade finds me attractive. He wants me, even with all my imperfections. He accepts me, and he desires me for who I am, what I look like. I never thought something like this would be possible after the accident.

"I can't believe you went out by yourself," says Suzie, clasping my hand. "I know it must have been terrifying, but I'm really proud of you." She shrugs. "Maybe it was a good thing I was too busy having lousy sex to answer your call. This was a big step. Now, we just have to work on getting you comfortable so you can stop wearing that mask."

Even though I've revealed my face to Kade, I'm not prepared to take off my mask for anyone else, even Suzie. I still wear it around the house.

"But still," says Suzie, shaking her head. "You're paying me to be at your beck and call, and I wasn't. I'm sorry."

I see by the look on her face that Suzie feels terrible. I tell her Mingus and I are okay now, hoping it makes her feel better. "He just got a tube sock lodged in his throat, and the doctor removed it." I scratch Mingus's head and he happily yips. "Anyway," I tell her, "You have a life to live, too. I can't expect you to be at my beck and call every minute of every day."

Suzie shoots me a surprised look. "Excuse me. Did you get kidnapped by aliens on your way to the animal hospital last night?" She giggles in disbelief. "You gave me a raise five months ago, so I would *always* be at your beck and call."

I shrug. Then, with a hint of a smile that Suzie can't see, I reply, "Well, maybe it's time I start doing some things for myself."

Suzie's jaw drops. She shakes her head. "Okay, you're definitely not telling me the whole story. What happened last night, besides taking Mingus to the hospital? After Kade got you out of there? I assume you guys fucked again. But that's not all. Is it?"

Suzie had seen some of the coverage online and all over the social media networks this morning. The news had broken that Kade had come to my rescue at the animal clinic.

I blush. I'm grateful the mask hides my emotion. Suzie shoots me an imploring look. She wants all the details. I'm about to tell her what happened when the buzzer at the front gate goes off.

Annoyed, Suzie hands Mingus to me and gets up from the couch. She walks to the intercom on the wall and presses the button.

"Hello?"

"It's Randy. Let me in." She sounds angry.

Suzie looks at me. I nod. "Let her in."

She presses the button on the intercom. A few minutes later, Randy storms into my living room. She shoots me a glaring look and snatches the TV remote from my hand. She flips the channel to the Star Central Network.

I've never seen Randy this angry, and I mean, never.

"What's wrong?" I ask, getting up from the sofa with Mingus in my arms. She holds up her hand, indicating I'm not to speak. She raises the volume on the television. All three of us gather in front of the large screen as footage of my visit to the animal hospital plays in front of us.

"Reclusive pop star, Melody Swanson, was seen late last night leaving her mansion and racing to a local animal hospital. Star Central has confirmed that the pop star's puppy, an English bull dog, was ill. The dog is doing fine now."

I glance at Mingus, who is resting in my arms, and scratch his head. "I think you've gotten me into a little bit of trouble," I mutter. He licks my fingers. I'm so grateful he's okay.

I turn my attention back to the television. The reporter continues giving a blow-by-blow account of my trip to the vet. Even with all the problems that exist in the world, it appears people are extremely interested in my sighting.

"Our sources report that Swanson appeared in a frenzied state at the animal hospital," continues the reporter.

"I wasn't that frenzied," I mumble.

"Shhh," says Randy. Her eyes are fixated on the TV. Her demeanor is very serious, focused. Suzie and I exchange a look. Randy is on edge; and as the news reporter keeps talking, we find out why.

"But it appears the pop star, who suffered a horrifying accident a year ago and currently wears a mask, was calmed down by the presence of a man named Kade Turner. Mr. Turner arrived at the animal hospital and helped escort Melody and her puppy away from reporters that had descended onto the scene."

"How did they get his name?" I ask.

"That's not all they got," snaps Randy.

My stomach drops as we continue watching the broadcast.

"Our investigative unit here at Star Central has

discovered that Mr. Kade Turner is a veteran who is currently employed as an escort. It appears he has been making frequent trips to Melody Swanson's mansion over the last several weeks. We have reached out to Miss Swanson's music label and agent for comment. And we're currently awaiting a reply."

Randy turns the television off. She sighs then turns to me with a look of bitter disappointment. "When I first saw the pictures of this guy leaving your place, I didn't ask any questions because I wanted to give you some space. But if I had known what he did for a living… an escort, Melody? Seriously? This is bad. You're supposed to be America's sweetheart. The label is furious."

"Well, tell the label if it wasn't for Kade, there wouldn't even be a new album."

"That's not the point," snaps Randy.

I lower Mingus to the floor and place my hands on my hips. "You know what? Fuck this America's sweetheart bullshit. I've been alone for over a year, and I've been miserable. He's the best thing that's happened to me."

"He's an escort!" shouts Randy.

"So what? If I were a guy, this wouldn't even be a story. All these male musicians get to fuck whoever they want."

"But you're not a guy," snaps Randy. "Your Melody Fucking Swanson. Mothers' take their daughters to your shows. Tickets for your next tour are about to go on sale. The label is worried there might be a boycott."

"Well, I didn't want to do this tour anyway," I exclaim.

Randy shakes her head in frustration. "You don't get it, Melody. The venues are already booked. The label has spent a ton of money. If your shows get boycotted, the label has already threatened to sue you for intentionally trying to sabotage your own tour."

"That's the most ridiculous thing I've ever heard," I shout.

Randy shrugs. "Maybe. But I just got off the phone with Jack, the president. If we don't figure out a way to contain this, they'll proceed with litigation."

"I fucking hate this label," I hiss.

"What are we going to do?" asks Suzie, worried.

Randy takes a deep breath. "I have an idea," she eventually says. "You're going to address the media."

"No fucking way!" I snap.

Randy holds up her hands. "Hear me out. Not like a press conference. It can just be a video you record on your phone. We do it right here in the living room. Now. We'll upload it. On the video, you're going to say that during a moment of weakness, because of the horrifying accident you've been through, and the loneliness and pain you've suffered as a result, you enlisted the services of someone to keep you company. It was a mistake and a decision you regret. You hope your fans can forgive you. You really want to put this unfortunate misstep behind you. You look forward to stepping out of the shadows and singing your music for your adoring fans that have helped you overcome such a difficult time."

"But I don't regret anything about Kade," I yell. "He saved me. My music. If it wasn't for him, there wouldn't be any new songs for my fans to love."

"This is about perception, Melody, not reality," replies Randy.

"I can't do it," I say, shaking my head. "I won't do it. Kade's helped me so much."

"Then do it for him," pleads Randy. "We need to contain the story now and get public opinion on our side. Otherwise, this is going to blowup. The media is going to hound this guy nonstop, like you've been hounded for the past year. Do you really want to put him through that? He didn't sign up for this. It's not fair to him. He has a regular life. Have you checked with him if he wants his life turned upside down by the fuckin' paparazzi?"

I remember telling Kade there was a risk he could become fodder for the media. But as Randy paints the picture of how bad it could get, I feel terrible. She's right. Kade didn't ask for this. Unfortunately, it's something I have to deal with in my profession. But Kade has no interest in the celebrity lifestyle or the media.

"What's the end game here, Melody?" Randy asks. "Because if you keep seeing this guy, you stand to lose everything. And his life will be made a living hell."

There's a long silence. I don't want to make Kade's life anymore painful than it already has been. I know first hand how cruel and disrespectful the paparazzi can be.

"If I do this video, do you think they will really leave him alone?" I ask.

Randy nods. "It's our best chance. If we can get the public on our side, and have them sympathize with you, then I don't think they'll bother him. Sure, they might follow him around for a couple of days. But if he's not a talker, they'll just move onto the next story. The key here is to emphasize that you regret your actions. Admit you've made a mistake, and you're asking for forgiveness."

"But I didn't make a mistake," I repeat. "He helped me."

Randy looks at me and sighs. "He's an escort, Melody. You paid someone for sex. Perception is reality. If you don't do this, the label will financially destroy you. And this guy, that you care so much about, will be on every trashy entertainment news outlet in the country, maybe even the world. His whole life, his entire backstory, will be put out there for everyone to see."

32

KADE

I'm lying in bed thinking about Melody again. This isn't about sex anymore. I'm feeling something more than just desire for her. But how could someone like me be with someone like her? I'm Shane's whore for crying out loud. She's a huge celebrity.

The only way I can be with Melody is if I'm my own man again. I need to stop being Shane's slave. I need my life back. I need my gym.

Even though it pains me, I decide to throw the fight.

My cellphone rings. I quickly answer, hoping it's her. But it's my sister, Layla.

"You're all over the news, Kade. Is it true? Are you an escort?"

I guess what Melody mentioned about the paparazzi has finally come to pass. This entire time, I've kept my arrangement with Shane a secret from my sister. I told Layla that Shane just wanted my gym in exchange for the money. Now, she finally knows the whole truth.

"It was part of the deal with Shane," I tell her with a sigh. "I was embarrassed to tell you."

"Is that the reason you never come around anymore?"

"Part of it," I admit.

"I'm your sister, Kade. You should have told me."

"Sorry," I mutter.

"Have you seen the video?"

"What video?" I ask, surprised.

"The video that Melody made."

"I didn't know she made a video."

"I'll send it to you now."

I get off the phone with Layla. Within a few seconds, I receive a text with a link to a video clip. Standing in my shitty studio apartment, I stare at my cellphone and see Melody's face. She's wearing her mask, something I had hoped she would stop doing after last night. As I listen to the video clip, I realize Melody has bigger issues to deal with.

"I want to apologize to all my fans," she says in the video, her voice trembling. "In a moment of weakness, I made a mistake. Please forgive me. The one thing I do not want to lose is the love and adoration my fans have given me throughout the years. If you all didn't stick by me, I don't think I would be able to step on stage again. My interactions with Mr. Turner occurred during a moment of loneliness. But now that I have music back in my life, I can leave that dark period behind and move forward to the next stage."

I stop the video and toss my phone onto the nightstand. I take a seat on the bed. I knew something like this might eventually happen. Melody warned me about it. I'm just surprised by how much it stings. I don't care that people know that I'm an escort. I just want to know the truth: am I a mistake she made in a moment of weakness? I can't be. Not after everything she told me. She said I saved her.

Last night didn't feel like a mistake. If anything, it proved to me that Melody and I were brought together for a reason. After Max died, I never thought I'd be happy again. When I made love to her at the gym, that's exactly how I felt. Happy. The sadness and depression I've been carrying inside me for so long were far off in the distance. As I held Melody in my arms, kissed her face, ravished her body, the sense of joy and gratitude flowing through me was overwhelming. Now, I'm wondering if it was all an illusion. Maybe Melody was acting. Maybe she was using me for what she needed, like so many of these Hollywood celebrities. And now, she's finished with me.

I laugh sarcastically to myself. What was I thinking? Someone with my background could never be with a woman like her. Not in a real way. She hired me to fuck her. And I let myself get caught up in the emotion. I was stupid. I should've known better. I should have never opened up to her.

My cell phone rings. I reach over and grab it from the nightstand. It's her.

I don't want to answer but know I must. "Hello."

"Hi," she says, her tone soft yet nervous. It kills me how much I love the sound of her voice. I'm going to miss it, because I know what this phone call is about before she utters another word.

"Something's happened," she says.

"Yeah," I reply, "I've heard."

There's a long silence.

"I saw your video clip," I tell her.

She takes a moment before responding. I can tell she's searching for the words. "My agent made me do it," she confesses.

"So, does that mean I'm not a mistake?"

"Of course not," she blurts. "You're the best thing that could've happened to me."

Upon hearing those words, my chest tightens. Fireballs of emotion surge up my throat. I want to tell her that she's the best thing that could've happened to me too. After being with her, I've realized my life still has meaning.

But then she starts talking, and I never get the chance to tell her how I feel.

"That's why it's so hard for me to say what I'm about to say, Kade."

Here it comes: the knockout blow.

She takes a deep breath. The moment seems to last forever.

"I have to stop seeing you, at least for a little while," she finally declares. I hear the sadness, the regret in her voice. "With all the venues for my tour already booked, the record label is threatening to sue me if people start boycotting my shows. That's why I made that video. My agent hopes it can stop the story from getting any bigger."

Although I understand why she needs to stop seeing me, it still hurts.

"I understand," I mutter. I want to say more but I just can't find the words.

There's another long silence. I hear her breathing

softly.

"I never thought this would happen," she says.

"That someone found out I'm a whore?" I reply. "You had said that was a possibility."

"No," she says with a sigh. "That you and me…" She takes a moment. "If it wasn't for you, Kade, I don't think I would…"

It's strange to hear her at a loss for words. She's a poet after all. "Yeah. You helped me out too," I whisper, realizing she feels the same way. This wasn't an illusion. What happened between us was real.

We were falling in love.

"I'm going to miss you," she confesses.

"Me too," I say softly.

There's a long silence. Neither one of us wants to get off the phone because we know it might be the last time we might talk.

"I want to wire you the next two hundred thousand."

I cringe. Money is the reason we can't be together. I'm a whore, and she paid me to fuck her. We just never imagined it would become much more than that.

"You don't have to do that."

"I want to," she replies. "I know the money can help you start a new life. You can get out of the debt you're under. It's the least I can do after everything you've done for me. Please don't refuse it."

"Thank you."

"There's one more thing," she says. "I have to warn you: you might get hounded by the press for a couple of days. Randy says if you don't talk to them this should all blow over soon."

"It won't be a problem. I won't talk to them."

Another long silence

"Thank you, Kade." Her voice is cracking. She's on the verge of tears. "You saved me."

Then, she hangs up.

"You saved me too," I mumble to myself.

I throw my cell phone against the wall. It shatters.

I look at the cracked and peeled ceiling. I fist my hands in a rage and punch the wall. I'm angry. I'm angry at myself for missing her already.

33

KADE

I guess it's a good thing I live in the ghetto. Even though the paparazzi want to talk to me, they don't want to take any risks by driving into my hood. Unfortunately, my gym is in a nicer section of town. So when I show up this morning, the parking lot is swarming with people. As I get out of my piece-of-shit Corolla, reporters and paparazzi pound me with questions. I don't answer any of them. As I unlock the door, I tell them to go fuck themselves. I am never going to talk. Then I turn and walk into the gym.

They don't get the hint.

Three hours later, they're still hovering outside, and I'm the only one in the gym. I guess nobody wants to deal with a mob of paparazzi on their way to a workout. I can't blame them.

I take advantage of the downtime by getting in a workout. Since I have nobody to spar with, I do some cardio and weight training. It feels good to unleash some of the anger that has built up inside of me.

I move to the punching bag and unleash a fury of kicks and jabs. My muscles burn and sweat pours down my face. I'm like a raging bull, mad at everything and everyone. I'm mad at the paparazzi and reporters swarming my gym. Melody and I should be none of their business. I'm mad at Shane for asking me to throw a fight, something I never thought I'd do. And most of all, I'm mad at Melody, for meeting her, getting to know her, and falling for her. Then I get angry with myself because I should've known better. I should never have let my emotions get the better of me.

I unleash one last round of kicks and jabs on the punching bag. Then, I stop to catch my breath. The front doorbell jingles, and I am shocked to see my sister, Layla, walk in. I smile as she approaches me. It's nice to see a friendly face.

"What are you doing here?" I ask.

"I've been calling you. You haven't been answering."

"I broke my phone."

"Ah, I see. Well, I stopped by your place and you weren't there. So I came here." She turns and glances at the reporters still hovering in the parking lot. "How long have they been here?"

"All morning," I reply. "You didn't talk to them, did you?"

Layla shakes her head. "I have nothing to say to them."

"Good," I say with a nod. "If they don't get any info, I'm hoping they'll disappear."

I notice Layla staring at me, annoyed. "I'm pissed at you."

"Why?"

"Because you weren't honest with me from the

beginning. How come you didn't tell me, Kade?"

"About me and Melody?"

She shakes her head. "About what Shane was making you do?"

I shrug. "I told you already. Being a whore is not exactly something you brag about, is it?"

She sighs then says, "Fine, but no more secrets. What about you and Melody?"

"What about us? It's over."

"Is that why you're trying to shred that punching bag?"

"I don't want to talk about it."

Layla holds up her hands. "Fine. Men are so annoying," she says.

Then she looks at me. I can tell by the expression on her face that she's struggling with something.

"What is it?"

Layla takes a few steps toward me. "Monique showed up to the house last night," she finally says. "She's been trying to find you."

I don't know how to respond. When Max was in the hospital and asked to see his mother, I tried to fulfill his wish and even enlisted Shane's help to find her. But after an extensive search, it looked like Monique had disappeared, vanished. Her parents knew nothing of her whereabouts. Word on the street was that her drug addiction had grown so bad, so life-threatening, that she was probably dead.

"Where has she been this whole time?"

"Detroit," answers Layla. "Sounds like things got pretty bad."

"How is she?" I ask.

I notice a small, sad smile cross my sister's lips. "She's clean. She's found God."

"At least one of us has," I mutter.

Then Layla takes a breath. "I told her I'd get in touch with you, and I'd let you know she's back in town." Sadness sweeps through my sister's eyes. She sighs and says softly, "Monique said she can't wait to see Max."

The wind gets knocked out of me. I look at the ground. Monique doesn't know Max has passed away.

Layla places a hand on my shoulder.

"I have to tell her," I sigh.

Layla nods. "Since I couldn't get a hold of you on your cell phone, I told Monique where you lived. She's probably going to stop by."

I inhale deeply. Seeing Monique is going to drag up all these feelings, feelings I've been trying to bury for so long. But I know I have to face them. Monique may have abandoned her child, but she has a right to know what happened to Max.

"Fuck, this is going to be tough," I mutter softly.

Layla squeezes my shoulder. "You're built for it, Kade."

Before Layla leaves, she makes me promise to come by her house for dinner. "Your nephews want to see you."

"I will," I reassure her. "After the next fight."

Layla smiles and before she goes says, "Knock him out, brother."

I don't have the heart to tell her the truth: I'm throwing the fight.

34

KADE

The warehouse is packed. It's a full house. Tickets cost three times the normal price. It appears my notoriety as Melody's escort has made this a must-see fight. I've heard there are even some reporters in the audience. Shane must be happy with the turnout. Since the bookies have me winning this fight – and Shane is betting against me – he stands to make a fortune.

I lost my fight against Jose Silva because I was angry and couldn't control my emotions. Instead of thinking about my next move, my mind was on Max. Right now, standing in this cage, about to square off against a solid fighter named Enrique Rosa from San Diego, I'm still angry. But my anger is focused. This poor dude standing in front of me doesn't know what he's up against.

I've had everything taken away from me that I've loved: my son, my gym, and Melody. Now, Shane is asking me to sacrifice the only thing that remains in my life – besides my sister – that I hold dear. I love to fight because there is honesty and truth in the cage. There is nowhere to run, all your illusions are stripped away. In the heat of a fight, and the crushing blow of a moment, you discover what you're made of. Outside the cage, in the bullshit society we've created for ourselves, the truth is sometimes hard to see. But inside the octagon, with a crowd screaming for blood, and the smell of sweat and fear in the air, the truth is facing you, as clear as day. If you're the fastest, the quickest, the smartest, and you don't lose your cool, you'll survive. You'll be the victor.

What Enrique Rosa doesn't know, as he takes a few steps toward me, is that I see the truth staring straight at me. If I throw this fight, I'll lose the one thing I believe in: the honesty of the cage. But not only that, I'd also be letting Max down. It would be as if I had taken my own life after he died. If I throw this fight, I won't respect myself. And when a man can't look himself in the mirror, what's the point?

Fuck Shane. Fuck money.

If he wants to kill me once the fight is over, I'm ready to die. Because the honor of the fight is all I have left to live for. Everything else has been taken from me.

As I take a few steps toward my opponent, one thing is obvious: I'm not losing, not today.

Enrique starts with some jabs to my body and my face. But I take a quick step back and surprise him with a roundhouse kick, throwing him off balance.

The crowd erupts in applause.

I lunge forward, hit him with a left hook, a quick jab to the body, then hurt him upstairs. I take a step back and nail him with a strike to the liver.

At that moment, everything goes into slow-motion. It's like I see his moves before they happen. I can react accordingly. I duck or slide out-of-the-way every time he's about to make impact.

After I land a few more blows, Enrique begins to tire out. He's waiting for the round to come to an end so he can catch his breath. I take advantage of the opportunity and knock him with a flying knee. He falls to the ground.

The crowd cheers. I turn and face them. Shane is staring straight at me, and I can tell he's pissed.

"Finish him!" I hear people shout.

I turn and watch Enrique slowly get up from the ground. He's got a busted lip and his chin and chest are covered in blood.

I run forward, lunge into the air, and pound him with a superman punch. He falls back to the ground. I unleashed a fury of punches – a clinical ground-and-pound – till I'm able to place him in a submission hold. Then he taps out.

The fight lasts a total of three minutes.

Poor Enrique never stood a chance.

The crowd erupts in thunderous applause and chants my name, "Kade! Kade! Kade!" But all I'm focused on is Shane. He's staring at me with disgust. He turns his back to me and walks out of the warehouse, Vince and Leo following close behind.

I may have won this fight, but in all likelihood I'm a dead man.

35

KADE

By refusing to throw the fight, I've undermined Shane. After all, there's one thing Shane values above all else: money. Even though I saved his life when we were kids, I think in Shane's mind that debt was wiped clean when he paid for Max's medical bills.

So now I'm waiting… waiting for the knock at my door, waiting for Shane and his two henchmen to drag me away and put a bullet in me. I wonder if I'll see my boy, Max, in heaven… if that's where I go.

When you're waiting for your death, it gives you time to reflect on your life. And when I look at the sum total of my existence, I'm filled with regret. I could have done better – as a father, and definitely as a person. That's why I got so angry when things with Melody ended. When I was with her, I felt like I was being a better version of 'me'. I was improving her life by being in it. So when she cut the cord and ended our relationship, I felt cast adrift.

I've been floating at sea ever since.

The knock finally comes. I sit up in bed and take a deep breath. I slide open the drawer of my nightstand and stare at my gun. After Max's death, I've put the muzzle of that gun in my mouth several times, struggling to pull the trigger. Now, I have a decision to make. Do I put up a fight against Shane? Or just take what's coming my way?

I decide to leave the gun in the drawer and slide it shut.

There's another knock. I slowly rise. My time is finally up. I take another deep breath and answer the door. My eyes widen.

It's not Shane standing before me…

It's Monique.

I hardly recognize her. She's dressed in a buttoned-up white blouse and black slacks. Her long dark hair is pulled back in a ponytail. When she sees me, she immediately looks at the ground, nervous. Then she gathers the courage to look up and half-smiles.

"Hey Kade," she says softly.

"Hey," I whisper in a daze. The last time I saw Monique, she was hollow-eyed, with sunken cheeks. Her voice was on edge, and her shivering body badly in need of a fix. The woman standing before me is a far cry from that memory. Monique looks healthy. Her cheeks are rosy, and her eyes are bright.

"You look great," I comment.

She nods slowly. "Thank you." Then she adds sadly, "It's taken me a long time to get myself together."

We stare at each other in silence. There are a million things I want to say to her, but I don't know where to start.

"How's Max?" she asks.

I look at the ground and sigh. Now, I know exactly

where to begin.

"You better come in, Monique. I have something to tell you."

After the initial shock, Monique's face turns pale. Tears form in her eyes, and she starts crying in pain. She curls herself into a ball and lies on my bed. I lie next to her and wrap my arms around her trembling body. I try to comfort her as best I can.

"I didn't deserve him," Monique cries through her tears. "I was such an awful mother, and he was such a good boy. I'm the one who should be dead. Not him. He did nothing wrong. I'm the sinner."

Monique sobs uncontrollably. I try to soothe her but realize she needs to release all this grief – just like I did when I listened to Melody's song.

"I tried to find you; but you disappeared," I tell her.

Monique continues crying. I don't know what to do. I just cradle her in my arms. With some time, she calms down. She wipes her nose and turns to me. Her eyes are puffy and red.

"We didn't deserve him," she repeats.

I nod. "I know. He was perfect."

Monique turns away and stares into nothingness.

Almost an hour passes as the two of us lie together in sad silence. Eventually, I get up from the bed and enter the bathroom. I splash some water on my face. Then, I step into the kitchen and pour Monique a glass of water. I return to the bed and hand it to her. She takes the glass and slowly sits up. She wipes her eyes and guzzles down the water. She places the empty glass on my nightstand.

She looks at me and asks, "Where's he buried?"

"With my parents," I tell her.

She slowly nods.

"I'd like to see him," she says quietly.

"I'll drive you."

We drive most of the way to the cemetery in silence. Monique just stares out the windshield, numb.

"He would have been proud of you," I tell her. "For getting clean. I am."

Monique looks at me. Her eyes are filled with regret. She sighs. "I never thought it would happen to me, Kade – that I'd become an addict. I just felt so alone, so much pressure. I was raising Max on my own, with no help. You were away in Iraq. I'm not making excuses. I let myself go there. I put myself before my son. Finding the next fix became more important than him. I wasn't thinking right. But I was just so miserable, Kade. When you came back, you were like a zombie. You didn't want anything to do with us."

I nod. "I know. I'm sorry." It still pains me to remember how I was back then.

Monique sighs again. "We were both fucked up in our own way. That's why I'm so angry that Max is the one that got taken. It should have been me, or you, not him. Not him."

She's overwhelmed again and begins to cry.

I reach across the car seat and hold her hand.

She continues to whimper on the way to the cemetery.

After parking the car, I hold Monique's hand as we

walk among the tombstones. When we get to Max's burial spot, she steps forward and kneels down. She kisses Max's gravestone. I hear her mumble softly, "I'm so sorry, sweetie. I'm so sorry." She begins to cry again.

When I think the time is right, I step forward and help Monique get up. Holding her, I walk her back to the car.

Inside, we sit in silence. Then Monique says, "We have to make him proud, Kade. You and I are still here for a reason."

"Sometimes I have a hard time believing that's true," I confess to her.

That night, Monique stays over. She has nowhere else to go. We share the same bed but that is all. There's only sadness and regret between us now.

The following morning, she asks if I can drop her off at Union Station so she can catch a bus back to Detroit.

"What's in Detroit?" I ask her on the way there.

"My church," she replies. Then she glances at me. "You should go sometime, Kade. It helps. I'm a volunteer."

"I do go to church," I tell her. "Except mine doesn't have any pews. It's the cage."

She smiles softly. At Union Station, I pay for her bus ticket. Before she boards, she turns to me and surprises me with a kiss goodbye on the lips.

"Take care of yourself," she whispers.

"You too."

As we stare at each other, I realize I may never see her again.

I hug her and say, "I'm so proud of you for getting clean."

"I'm going to stay clean, for Max," she replies.
Then she boards the bus and leaves.

36

KADE

I'm back at the gym. The media people that were gathered outside have left. Someone mentioned that one of those famous reality TV sisters was found having a threesome at an amusement park. With another story to follow, the swarm of paparazzi bees took off. My fifteen minutes of fame have gratefully come to an end. So, too, has the boycott of my gym. With the reporters and paparazzi gone, many of my clients return.

I fall back into my routine of managing the gym and training clients. I still haven't seen Shane. It's been five days since the fight, and I thought I'd be dead by now. After Monique left, I decided not to wait around for Shane to knock on my door. So, I went back to work. I wasn't going to run from him. Shane knew where he could find me.

I'm instructing that young kid, Rico, on the finer points of a double leg takedown. Luke, one of my trainers, is helping me demonstrate. The double leg takedown is a basic move but always effective.

"Put your lead foot between your opponent's legs," I tell Rico as I demonstrate on Luke. "Then, drop your knee to the floor. But make sure it's behind his leg. Now you have to slide around your opponent's legs and wrap your arms around the back of his knees. Then step forward with your trailing leg and get onto your feet." Holding Luke's legs, I get up and knock him off balance. He crashes to the mat. Then I quickly pin him.

I look up at Rico. "Ready to give it a try?"

He nods. "Yeah. I think so."

I get off Luke and offer him a hand up. "Give it a try on Luke."

Rico steps forward and practices the move.

"Good," I say as Rico takes Luke down. "Keep pressure on his torso with your shoulder when you got him down. Try it again."

Rico and Luke get back on their feet. That's when I see him. Shane is standing by the front door with Vince and Leo behind him. Slowly, he walks toward me. His eyes are steady, his face expressionless.

Shane snarls at Rico, "Lesson's over, kid."

Rico looks at me and I nod.

I order Luke, "Clear out the gym."

"You sure, boss?" he asks, shooting me a worried look.

I nod. "Do as I say, Luke. Clear it out."

Luke walks around the gym and tells everyone to leave. When my customers get the stare down from Vince and Leo, they get the hint, anyway. While this is going on, Shane and I just stare silently at each other. So, this is how it's going to go down… in my gym. In a way, it's sort of fitting.

When the last person leaves the gym, and the doorbell

jingles behind him, Shane finally speaks. His voice is calm and even.

"These last couple of days, I've been doing a lot of thinking, Kade."

I don't respond.

Shane begins to walk around the gym, stopping when he reaches the punching bag. He presses his hand against it – pushes it – so that it begins to sway. Then he glances at me. "You didn't run."

"I've got nowhere to go," I reply. "This gym is all I have."

"Too bad I own it," Shane taunts.

He walks toward me. He eyes Vince and Leo and nods. The two of them start pulling down the window shades, and they lock the front door.

"You should've skipped town, Kade." He walks up to me and whispers, "Now, you've put me in a tough spot."

"You've got to do, what you've got to do," I tell him, looking him straight in the eyes.

For a brief second, I think I see some sympathy, but then it disappears. Shane takes a deep breath and nods. "I lost a lot of money on that fight."

"You want to add that to my tab?" I reply.

He looks at me, smirks, and then hits me with a left. My jaw stings. I'm about to swing back, but his henchmen pull out their guns.

"Not yet!" shouts Shane as he massages his hand. I guess it hurts from hitting me.

He takes a deep breath and exhales through his nostrils. He stares at me and huffs. "Kade, I'll be honest with you. I don't want to kill you. You saved my life when we were kids. And on top of that, you're one of my best whores. But you can't disrespect me and expect to get away with it."

I sigh. "Shane, fighting is all I have. I've lost everything else. I couldn't throw the fight."

He looks at me and sighs. Then he wags his finger and says, "That's some sentimental bullshit, dude. What good is honor if you can't even feed yourself?"

I don't bother to reply. Shane and I see the world differently. We always have and always will. In his view, it's kill or be killed, make money or lose money. Everything is black and white, and there's no room for grey.

"You still seeing that burned-up chick?" he asks.

"No."

"She pay up?"

I nod. "I got two hundred grand."

That gets his attention. "It's yours," I declare.

He nods. "Good. That should settle all of Max's medical bills." He looks at me. "You and I would've been square if you didn't let your sense of honor get in the fucking way, Kade. Why'd you have to be such a fuckin' idiot? I was about to give you back your gym. But then you go and fuckin' disrespect me by not throwing the fight."

"I told you. It wasn't about disrespecting you. It had nothing to do with you."

"I lost three hundred grand because of you!" he shouts.

"And I took a bullet in my back to save your life," I comeback, staring him straight in the eyes.

He doesn't respond. He just keeps looking at me. I can tell he's trying to figure out what to do. He glances down at the ground and takes a breath. Then he looks at me and shrugs.

He pulls out his gun.

37

Melody

I can hear the audience outside my dressing room. They're chanting my name. Randy is ecstatic; the Forum is sold out.

"I told you they'd forgive you," she says, beaming. I stare at her reflection in my dressing room mirror. I feel sick.

She squeezes my shoulders.

"Now, just remember to thank the fans for all their support while you were recovering. And thank the label too, if you can. I want to make sure we stay on their good side."

"Randy, why couldn't we have started with a small show? I'm not even comfortable leaving my house yet and I'm performing my first show at the Forum? This is crazy," I complain. "Why couldn't we have done something at the Whiskey A Go-Go or a smaller venue? There are over 17,000 people out there, Randy. I'm not ready."

"We didn't have a choice," says Randy staring back at my reflection. "The label–"

I hold up my hand, cutting her off. "Enough with the

fuckin' label!" I shout, shaking my head.

Randy squeezes my shoulders, trying to calm me down. "Once you're out there, you'll feel comfortable again. You're just having some jitters."

I shrug her off. I'm annoyed and wracked with nerves.

"I'm going to have 17,000 people scrutinize me," I tell her. "They're going to take pictures of me. Then they're going to inspect the photos, analyze the scars on my hands, my neck. Then the reviews are going to come in. The comments will be focused on my mask and how I carried myself after the accident. My entire being will be dissected after this first show… scrutinized, critiqued."

I feel tension forming in my chest. That queasy sensation in my stomach grows.

I don't want to deal with the negative comments, the hurtful statements about my appearance. Sure, people say not to pay attention to them. But with Twitter and Facebook, they're always there, just a click away. I'm not strong enough to face all of that. Not yet. I'm not ready. I know Kade said 'you're never ready', but my body is going into full-blown panic mode as I contemplate stepping on stage.

I feel like I'm about to vomit.

"Are you okay, Melody?" Randy asks.

I look at her and shout. "Leave!"

Randy looks at me, shocked. She slowly walks to the door.

Once she's gone, I stare at my reflection. I'm still wearing my mask, even though my last surgery has helped with most of the scarring. I'm just not comfortable taking it off in front of anyone… but him.

Randy says the label doesn't care if I wear the mask. They think it lends gravitas to my show.

The show.

I can't put on a show.

Not in front of all those people.

The thought brings on another wave of nausea, and that tightness in my chest intensifies. I try to calm down and control my breathing.

God, I wish he were here. Ever since our last phone conversation, I haven't been able to stop thinking about him. He's the only thing that seems real to me anymore. When I was with him, it was the only time I felt grounded and not afraid.

There's a knock at the door. "Five minutes," someone shouts.

I turn back to the mirror and fidget with my mask. My hands are shaking. I don't think I can go through with this. I don't think I can face them – all of them – staring at me. I start getting the shivers, and my whole body breaks out in a sweat. My breath catches in my throat.

"Four minutes," someone shouts.

The room begins to spin, my vision blurs.

There's another knock at the door. "Melody, do you need anything?"

I turn and see Suzie. I wave her to come in. She closes the door behind her.

"I can't breath," I manage to get out.

She rushes to my side. She kneels down and grabs my hands. She looks me straight in the eyes.

"You're having a panic attack," she says calmly.

"No shit," I say, still struggling for air.

"Look at me, Melody. Just take deep breaths with me. Here we go, one…"

Suzie takes a deep breath and I try to follow her, but then I shake my head.

"I can't do this, Suzie. I can't go out there."

"I know this is scary, Melody. But you can do this."

I vigorously shake my head. I feel myself tearing up, near hysterics.

"I can't."

"Yes -"

"I can't!" I shout. I beg her, "Please, Suzie. Get me out of here. Please."

She looks at me, concerned. "Are you sure, Melody?"

I nod. "I just want to go home," I cry. I sound like a scared little girl – which at this moment is exactly what I am.

"But there's a whole crowd – "

"I don't care," I say, cutting her off. "I can't face them. I'm not ready."

Suzie looks at me and realizes how serious this is. "Okay," she says softly. "There's going to be hell to pay but grab my arm."

Suzie helps me up, out of the chair. She grabs some of my things and walks me out of the dressing room.

She takes me home.

38

Melody

I'm curled up in bed, under the sheets. Mingus is by my side. I gently stroke his belly as I hear Randy and Suzie arguing outside my bedroom door.

"This is important. I need to talk to her."

"She needs her rest," I hear Suzie reply. "Can't we just deal with this tomorrow?"

Randy loses her temper. "We have 17,000 concert-goers demanding their money back!" I hear her shout. "We're all over the news! I just got off the phone with Jack at the label."

"What did he say?" Suzie asks, her tone worried.

"They're suing," snaps Randy. "They want Melody to be financially responsible for the loss of revenue tonight and any subsequent shows. Do you know how much tonight cost her? Four million dollars. We owe the label four million dollars! If Melody cancels the remainder of the shows – "

"I know," Suzie replies.

"That's almost fifty million dollars she's going to owe them!"

"I get it!" shouts Suzie. "I can do the math."

I slowly rub Mingus's back. He turns and licks my mask.

"We have to get her back on stage," Randy says, exasperated.

"Well, we can't drag her out there, Randy. She was in a full-blown panic attack in the dressing room. There was no way she was going to perform. I've never seen her like that…"

They keep talking but I zone out. My body is numb. I just want to stay under these bed sheets forever. Mingus stops licking my mask and rests his head on my shoulder.

"Can we stay here forever, Mingus?"

Mingus huffs.

Then there's a knock at the door.

"Melody, I'm coming in," Randy says.

The bedroom door opens and Randy steps in, followed by Suzie. I turn away from Mingus and look at her. She's trying her best to hide her disappointment in me, but it's not working.

"I'm sorry, Randy," I say. "I just couldn't go out there."

"But why?" she asks. "They all wanted you. They love the new songs. You were going to perform wearing the mask."

"I don't know. I just couldn't do it," I declare.

"If we don't work through this, Melody," says Randy, her voice now filled with concern. "You could go bankrupt. The label is going to hold you financially responsible for all the missed shows."

The thought frightens me. But not as much as stepping out on stage does.

I look at Randy and concede, "I think you should stop representing me, Randy. Because I'm finished."

"Really?" she replies.

I nod slowly.

Randy sighs. "I'm not giving up on you that easily. I'll come back tomorrow. Get some rest."

Suzie walks Randy out. I stay in bed, cuddling Mingus in my arms. I know I'm being a coward. But I'd rather die than go through what I experienced tonight... again.

Suzie knocks lightly on the bedroom door.

"What is it?"

She steps in and takes a seat on the bed. She looks at me, her eyes reflecting her worry.

"Can I get you anything?" she asks.

I shake my head. "I'm okay. You can go home."

She doesn't move. She glances at the ground, thinking.

"What is it?"

She shrugs. "I think you should call Kade."

I'm surprised to hear Suzie mention his name.

"Why?"

"He's the only one who's helped you get your confidence back. Maybe he can help you get over this hurdle."

"Suzie, you were there when we discussed this. We all agreed it was best to cut ties with him – for my reputation and his own peace of mind."

Suzie looks at me, her face serious. "After what happened tonight, your reputation doesn't matter, Melody. What matters is getting you out on stage. Randy's not exaggerating. You could owe the label fifty million dollars." She takes my hand and squeezes it. She looks me straight in the eyes. I see how genuine her concern for me is. "Melody, I can't imagine how scary this is for you. But we have to do something. I don't want to watch you lose everything you've worked so hard for. You have to get over this fear and maybe Kade can help."

"The escort comes to the rescue," I reply sarcastically.

"I realize, now, he was much more than that," Suzie admits.

"He was," I reply. "That's why I hate myself for ending it with him. It was the worst thing I've ever done."

Suzie lets go of my hand and stands up. "All I know, Melody, is that the clock is ticking. Maybe having Kade in your corner will help you."

"So, I just ring him up and ask if I can hire him again? See if he wants to go on tour with me, so I can overcome a serious case of stage fright?"

Suzie shrugs. "Maybe. Who knows? He might actually want to help. And besides, do you have any other ideas? Because if we don't do anything, you're going to be finished." She looks at me, and I see tears forming in her eyes. "And I really don't want to work for anyone else, Melody."

She turns away, embarrassed. "I'm sorry. But it's true. You're my best friend, and I love you. I don't like seeing you like this."

Wiping her eyes, she walks out of the room.

39

Melody

I call Kade's cellphone; but it goes straight to voicemail. I try again a few hours later, same thing. The following day, I call again and get an automated message: this mailbox is full. Did Kade lose his cell phone? Is that why he's not answering? Then a worrisome thought enters my mind: maybe something happened to him. I try to shove the thought away. I tell myself I'm overreacting. But that sense of worry creeps back into my stomach.

I lift Mingus into my arms and begin nervously pacing my house. "He's fine," I mutter out loud. "Just because his voicemail is full doesn't mean something happened to him."

Mingus barks.

"Don't say that," I respond.

He barks again.

I stop pacing and look at him, annoyed. "Shit Mingus, why'd you have to say that?"

He lets out a series of barks this time, getting his point across clearly.

"You're right. You're right," I concede. "I don't have a good feeling about this either."

Carrying Mingus in my arms, I hurry into the kitchen. I grab my keys from the kitchen counter and walk to my backdoor. I take a deep breath and open it.

"You better be alright, Kade," I ramble as I step into the sunlight. Sliding into my car, I place Mingus in the passenger seat. I stare at the gate at the end of my driveway. I place my sunglasses over my mask.

"Here we go." I start up the car and roll it toward the gate. I press the button on my remote. Just as I feared, as the gate slides open, a wave of reporters block my path with their cameras pointed straight at me. A cacophony erupts. Everyone wants to talk to me about canceling my show. The hysterical crowd shouts several questions at me. Then the reporters swarm my car, yelling, and shoving their cameras against my car windows. I honk my horn, trying to get them to move out of the way. Their shouting continues, and Mingus begins barking at them. It's utter chaos. I wave at the reporters to get out of my way. I don't want to run anyone over, or hurt anyone. But they won't budge. Slowly, I ease my car forward, and the crowd finally parts. I notice several reporters running to their cars, hoping to follow me. Once I feel it is safe, and realize I don't have much time to lose them, I slam on the accelerator and take off.

I'm rushing with adrenaline. The chaos outside my house has put me on edge. And the thought that something might have happened to Kade fills me with worry. I don't know where Kade lives, so I decide to go to his gym. I punch Kade's Cage into my phone and have the GPS direct me. In order to lose the paparazzi – that I'm sure are following me – I take several back roads.

All the commotion has excited Mingus, and he's jumping up and down in the passenger seat barking.

"I'm going as fast as I can, Mingus. I don't want to get into another accident."

He understands and finally calms down.

I check my rearview mirror. It looks like no one is following me. I breathe a sigh of relief.

When I finally get to Kade's gym, and pull into a parking spot, I realize how tense I am. My hands are gripping the steering wheel for dear life. "Please be in there," I whisper out loud. If something's happened to him – if he's gone – I don't know what I'll do. Now, it's crystal clear just how much he means to me.

In a short amount of time, he's become the one.

The one I want to wake up to.

The one I want to support.

The one I feel blessed to have in my life.

He better be okay. Because if he's not, I'm really going to lose it. My panic attack before the concert, or the suicidal depression I felt after my car accident, will pale in comparison to the pain I'll feel if the person I have fallen in love with, the one who gives me hope, has been snatched away from me.

I slide my sweaty hands off the steering wheel. Taking another deep breath, I open my car door. I get out, and Mingus immediately jumps into my seat and barks at me. He wants to come too. I grab him and slam the car door shut. I nervously walk toward the front door of the gym.

I swing the door open and immediately begin scanning the room. The gym is packed. But among the crowd of men and women, I don't spot Kade.

Mingus lets out a series of barks. I lower him to the ground and he takes off. In a frenzy, I walk around the gym, searching for Kade.

He's not among the people wrestling on the mats. He's not one of the dudes lifting weights. I don't see him working the punching bag. As I fear the worst, my heart pounds in my chest.

Is he gone? Could something have really happened to him?

In a daze, I continue searching the gym. I make my way toward the back, where the cage is. Then I hear Mingus loudly barking.

"What the fuck?" I hear a man shout. "Dude, what the fuck is a dog doing here?"

Mingus continues barking.

"Easy there," I hear someone say.

"Kade, he's attacking me!"

"Grow a pair. He's a puppy. You'll be fine."

I hurry toward the back of the gym. When I see the cage, I stop in my tracks. I found him.

Mingus is jumping around inside the cage. My face breaks into a smile as I watch Kade reach down and pick him up. Mingus begins licking his face. "Hey buddy," Kade says with a grin. "You've missed me, huh?"

"I have too," I say.

He looks in my direction. My heart is still pounding in my chest, but no longer with worry, with nervous excitement instead.

We stare at each other silently. He's okay. I'm so grateful he's okay.

Kade's face softens as he looks at me. His once haunted eyes, are smiling back at me.

As I take him in, I realize how much I love him.

Kade steps out of the cage and approaches me.

"I thought something crazy happened to you, like you might be dead," I tell him, the sense of relief still noticeable in my voice.

Kade nods with a warm smile as he stares at me. "I nearly was. But for a guy who hates talking, it turns out I'm not bad at persuading people."

"I could have told you that," I affirm.

Then I notice Kade's eyes narrow as he looks past me. The hard lines on his face reappear. He hands Mingus to me and races forward.

"Hey, Melody, are you and your boyfriend back together?"

I turn and see a camera lens pointed at me. Then I see his round, bearded face smirking at me from behind the camera. It's him: Charlie.

"Come on, Melody, the people have a right to know," he says taking a step forward, filming us.

"Leave her alone," Kade shouts.

The paparazzi points his camera at Kade.

"There he is," Charlie teases. "Kade Turner, Melody's favorite escort!"

"Get out of here," Kade barks. He shoves Charlie, and his large frame stumbles backward. But Charlie doesn't get the message. He moves forward, with his camera, and shoves it right in my face.

"Here for a quickie? Is that it, Melody? You can't perform for your fans. But you don't have a problem putting out for your boyfriend."

"Just leave us alone," I cry.

Mingus barks at him.

Charlie turns his camera back to Kade.

"You must really need the money, huh, Kade? How much does Melody pay you to have sex with her busted up body?"

Kade turns bright red and punches Charlie in the face. The camera flies out of Charlie's hands. He crashes to the floor. The paparazzi looks up, blood pouring out of his nose. I think Kade broke it. But Charlie doesn't look upset. In fact, he has a smile on his face. He wanted Kade to hit him!

"You just fucked yourself, dude." He smirks, pointing his finger at Kade. "I'm suing your ass for assault."

"Well, if that's the case," Kade replies. "Let me really fuck you up."

Charlie wasn't expecting that, his eyes widen with fear. He scrambles back as Kade lunges forward.

"Kade don't," I shout. I drop Mingus to the floor and run in between them.

"He can't talk to you like that," Kade hisses. His eyes are on fire. "I won't let anyone ever talk to you like that."

"Oh, I get it. He's not only your fuck toy but your bodyguard," Charlie says as he stands up. "You get a bonus for that, Kade?"

Kade wants to take another swing at Charlie, but I press myself against him. I grab his face with both my hands and stare deeply into his eyes. "Don't Kade. He's not worth it." Kade's eyes meet mine. He is full of rage. I try to calm him down. "He's not worth it," I repeat. His chest is heaving. He's so angry.

Then I hear Charlie talking into his cell phone. "Yes, is this the police? I'd like to report an assault."

I turn and stare at him. "Please, don't do that," I beg. "Please, don't press any charges."

Charlie shoots me a curious look. "Your boyfriend should learn to control his temper." He begins talking into his phone, "Yes, I'm at Kade's Cage. I've just been assaulted by the owner, and I'm worried for my safety."

I can't let this asshole press charges against Kade. This mess is my fault.

"What if I take off my mask?" I blurt.

Charlie turns and looks at me, shocked.

"Really?"

I slowly nod. "You'll get the exclusive on two conditions: you don't press any charges, and we never see you again."

Charlie ends his call. His face breaks out in a smile. "Deal," he replies.

"You don't have to do this, Melody."

Kade looks at me with concern.

"Yes, I do," I reply. I look into his eyes. I see a love so powerful. "For you, it's the least I can do," I admit.

He softly smiles.

I turn, face Charlie and say, "Okay, you sleazy son-of-a-bitch. Get your shot."

Charlie snatches his camera from the floor and points it at me. "No need for the name calling," he replies as he turns on the camera. "Alright, I'm ready. This is Charlie Winger with an exclusive. America's sweetheart, Melody Swanson, is about to reveal to the world the face she's been hiding for so long."

Staring into the camera lens, I take a deep breath. I slowly reach behind my head and begin loosening the straps of my mask. My heart races and my body trembles, as I slowly slip it off. Then I look up and stare into the bright light of the camera... exposed.

I breathe a sigh of relief.

I'm finally free.

Epilogue

Melody

One Year Later...

The last time I was in this dressing room, I was falling apart. I was gripped by a deadly fear that rocked me to my core. The thought of stepping on stage had become so terrifying; I believed I'd never be able to do it again.

A lot has changed since then.

I've performed eleven sold-out concerts throughout the country. My new album and tour are a qualified success. The reviews have been amazing and the support from the fans has been incredible. Sure, there have been some trolls on social media who make disgusting comments about my face. But now I see them for what they are: inconsequential. It was only by truly accepting my face and body for what it was – and not what I wished it to be – that I finally found the courage to just be me. In a strange way, I have that paparazzi motherfucker, Charlie, to thank for all this. When he threatened to press charges against Kade, I stopped thinking about myself. I wanted to do whatever I could to help Kade at that moment.

My love for him overpowered my fear.

Now, I'm back in the dressing room of the LA Forum. It's the last show of my tour – a make-up appearance for the one I canceled. I finish putting on my makeup and check my appearance in the mirror. The foundation helps hide the scarring. But it's still noticeable, especially when they flash an image of me on the huge monitors during the show. I'm not going to lie to you; the first time I saw my face plastered on that screen, I freaked out a bit. But the audience got me through it. They were cheering me on and singing my songs. They just cared about the music and not what I looked like.

I put on some mascara, then glance at Mingus. He's playing with a ball in the corner of the room.

"What do you think, Mingus?"

Mingus looks at me and barks.

"I think you're just being nice," I say with a smile. Mingus has been with me the entire tour. And this past year, he's gotten a lot bigger.

There's a knock at the door.

"Come in."

"Babe, the crowd out there is going crazy."

"Really?"

Kade nods. "They're really pumped."

The second he's in the room, Mingus darts toward Kade, wanting to play. "Hey buddy," Kade says as he rubs his coat. "I bet you're excited to finally be home, huh? Aren't you, boy?"

Mingus licks his dad's face and then hurries to fetch his ball. Kade walks over to me. He places his hands on my shoulders and stares at my reflection in the mirror.

"How about you, beautiful? You happy to be home?"

I turn in my chair and face him, grab hold of his hands. "You have no idea," I answer as I stand up.

I give him a long lingering kiss. "All I want," I tell him, "is to stay in bed with you for a week."

"Sounds like a plan," he says as he kisses me and squeezes my ass.

Mingus growls. We both look down and notice the tennis ball in his mouth. Kade grabs it and tosses it across the room. Mingus chases after it.

"I have a surprise for you," I tell Kade as I rest my hand against his chest.

"You back home with me is all I want," he whispers. He kisses me and tugs on my bottom lip.

I look into his eyes and can't believe how much I love this man. I'm so grateful to have him in my life. And he's made it irrefutable: how much he loves and cares for me.

"Just promise me, honey, you'll be near the stage during the show."

"Of course I will, babe. I'll be standing offstage just like you asked." He looks at me curiously. "Why? What's the surprise?"

"It won't be a surprise, if I tell you. Now, will it?"

Mingus growls again. He wants another round of

catch. Kade snatches the ball from his jaw and tosses it once more.

There's a knock at the door.

"Who is it?"

"It's Randy and Suzie. We need to talk."

The door swings open. Randy and Suzie enter, both beaming.

I notice Randy is walking a little gingerly.

"What's wrong with you?" I ask her.

Randy points her finger at Kade. "I started going to your boyfriend's gym. That's what's wrong with me. Luke, my trainer, might be gorgeous but he's a drill sergeant."

"No pain, no gain," says Kade with a smile.

Randy places a hand on Kade's shoulder. "Kade, sweetie," she says, shaking her head, "You need to talk to him." Randy then shoots me a look. "You realize he doesn't even let me answer my phone during our workouts? He says I can't learn how to kick box while having a conference call. Can you believe that?"

I look at Kade and grin. Kade just stands there, shaking his head at Randy.

"Kade, I saw your last fight in Chicago," says Suzie. "Is that poor guy alright?"

Kade nods. "Just a few bruised ribs. He wants a rematch."

"Melody, I don't know how you do it," says Suzie. "I was a nervous wreck watching him fight. I kept covering my eyes whenever he got punched or kicked."

"Well, just wait until Vegas next month," I reply. "There's nothing like watching him fight live."

Kade grins at me. He's fighting professionally again. And he is up for a championship fight next month in Vegas.

Shane is his manager.

Over a year ago, when Shane showed up to Kade's gym – looking to kill him – Kade talked him out of it. Kade told Shane that he wanted to see how far he could go in the cage. He wanted to fight professionally again. With Shane as his manager, they could make a lot of money. Apparently, there's nothing Shane likes more than money. And now that Kade is the hottest fighter on the circuit, Shane is raking it in.

Kade's even scheduled to do a commercial next week. He's dreading it. I'm giving him some pointers on how to act in front of the camera.

"I'll let you three talk business," Kade says. He looks at me and grins. He gives me another quick kiss. "Knock them dead, babe." He turns to Randy and Suzie. "I'll see you two at our place for dinner this week."

"See you, Kade." They both smile as he's about to leave.

"Remember what I told you," I shout at him before he closes the door.

Kade nods. "I'll be there the whole show, honey."

When he closes the door, I turn to Randy and Suzie. They're both still beaming.

"What is it?" I ask.

"I just got off the phone. The label wants to go worldwide," shouts Randy.

Suzie excitedly claps her hands. "You're back, Melody. You're better than ever."

I can't believe it. "Really? A worldwide tour?"

Randy nods. She's so excited she can hardly contain herself. "Your album is number one. And this tour is the hottest ticket of the summer. My phone hasn't stopped ringing. I'm getting calls for endorsements. Universal Studios just called. They want to know if you'd be interested in co-starring with Bradley Cooper in a new movie. Also, Taylor Swift wants to do a song with you, and so does Jay-Z."

I hold up my hand, trying to calm her down. "Randy, I need to take a break."

"What about the worldwide tour?" she asks.

I shake my head. "It will have to wait. I've fulfilled my obligation to the label. Now I need some time for myself."

She looks at me and slowly nods. "Alright," she replies, a little disappointed. "But can we at least squeeze in a commercial, and a Swift/Jay-Z collaboration?"

"Fine," I say, "But no world tour. Not yet."

Randy gives me a hug and a kiss on the cheek. "Okay, sweetie. Knock them dead tonight." She looks at me and says, "I'm so proud of you."

"Thanks."

Randy leaves.

Suzie, whose been playing in the corner with Mingus this whole time, looks at me.

"I'm so happy to be home."

"Me too," I agree with a sigh. The last year Suzie has been with me every step of the way.

"Are you sure you don't want to go to the after party?" she asks.

I nod. "I'm exhausted. I just want to go home and spend some time with my man."

Suzie shrugs and says, "I can't blame you."

"Five minutes!" the production manager shouts as he knocks on the door.

I take a deep breath and smile. "Okay, I got to go."

I walk over to Suzie and give her a hug. "Love you."

"Love you too," she says squeezing me back.

Mingus barks.

I rub his head. "I love you too, buddy."

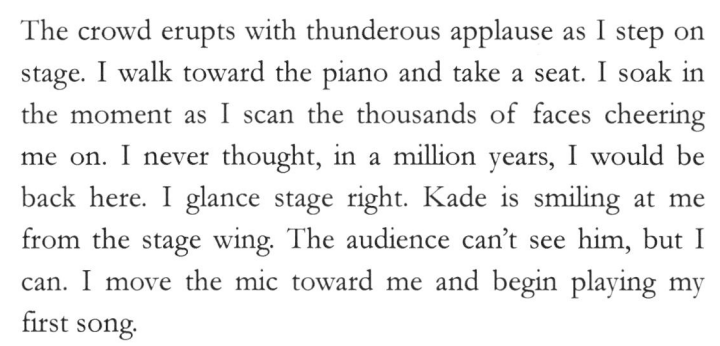

The crowd erupts with thunderous applause as I step on stage. I walk toward the piano and take a seat. I soak in the moment as I scan the thousands of faces cheering me on. I never thought, in a million years, I would be back here. I glance stage right. Kade is smiling at me from the stage wing. The audience can't see him, but I can. I move the mic toward me and begin playing my first song.

The audience is with me the entire night. They know the words to all my new songs. The amount of love I feel in the arena is overwhelming. And when I get to the last song of the night, I can hardly contain the emotions running through me.

"This is the last song for now," I speak into the mic. The crowd expresses their disapproval. "I know. I know. But it's time, unfortunately. Before I sing, though, I want to let you all know how much you mean to me. The last time I was here, I couldn't step out on stage. I was so scared. I was afraid of how I looked, what you all might think of me. I was paralyzed with fear. But sitting here now, I realize I had nothing to be frightened of. You have been wonderful. You've all stuck by me during a really difficult time and I want to thank you." The crowd cheers.

"There's one person in particular I want to single out. This person is the reason I even have songs to sing. He's the one who's inspired every song on my new album." I glance offstage and see Kade looking at me. "He's the love of my life." I swear I see Kade blushing as he glances at the ground. Then he looks back up at me. "But unfortunately, he's also the reason I won't be able to go on a world wide tour." The crowd begins booing. "Hey, that's not very nice," I say playfully to the audience. They let out a collective laugh. Then I turn and look at Kade, stare deep into his eyes. He's not sure what I'm talking about. I take a deep breath and continue. My eyes are fixated on his beautiful face the whole time. "You see, ladies and gentlemen, Kade and I are going to have a baby. I'm going to have a child with the love of my life."

The crowd erupts with joy. Kade's face breaks out in a grin. I get up from my piano and run toward him. He takes me in his arms.

"Really?" he asks.

I nod, looking at him. I see tears in his eyes.

"Are you happy?" I ask him.

"Happy?" he repeats. He shakes his head and takes my face in his hands. He kisses me. "I'm grateful, Melody. Grateful."

I hug him and we stare at each other. We both cry tears of joy.

Together, our future is bright.

Other Books by Ozlo & Priya Grey

"This is one dripping, delicious and salacious story of sexual awakening!" – *Obsessed with Myshelf*

"This is definitely a story about a BDSM Sexual, Erotic Awaking. It's also a story about a woman who has survived and is taking life by the balls!" – *Reading Keeps Me Sane*

Other Books by Ozlo & Priya Grey

"This book was fantastic and deeply emotional. It's breathtaking in its ability to make you feel the characters emotions...it pulls you in and takes you on an incredible journey of love surviving against all odds." – *Alphas Do It Better Book Blog*

"Three decades of finding love, loss, insecurities, heartbreak and finding yourself. This story had me in uncontrollable tears but made me realize to not take time for granted. 5 Star read!" – *Books, Wine and Lots of Time*

Other Books by Ozlo & Priya Grey

"Emotional, sexy and a wonderful read. The authors have done a brilliant job with the character development, mind blowing story and keeping the reader interested and wanting more with every page of reading it." – *SBB Reviews*

"A refreshing read. Thought it was the typical story line with the hot jock who falls for the shy girl. It was so much more… follows the story of four people which is really enjoyable to read. The characters all blend and connect in such a great way that you will find yourself involved in all stories. It was a great and surprising read."
– *Read, Love Blog*

About the Authors

Ozlo and Priya Grey collaborate to produce contemporary romance novels that are known to pull at your heartstrings while leaving you to contemplate life's greater purpose. They have authored four contemporary romance novels, including the Amazon #1 inspirational romance bestseller, *Healing Melody*.

Their time is consumed with developing stories for future projects, writing and re-writing, and tinkering with graphic design. When they step away from their desks, they enjoy watching movies and long walks on the beaches of Southern California.

Please visit Ozlo and Priya at www.ozloandpriya.com.

Printed in Great Britain
by Amazon